His Melody

TARA CONRAD

HIS ONE HER ONLY PUBLISHING

Copyright © 2024 by Tara Conrad

All rights reserved.

No part of this book may be reproduced in any form or by any electronic or

mechanical means, including information storage and retrieval systems, without

written permission from the author, except for the use of brief quotations in
a book

review.

Any reference to historical events, real people, or real places are used fictitiously.

Names, characters, and places are products of the author's imagination.

Published by: His One, Her Only Publishing

Cover Art by: Boundless Book Covers

Formatting by: Mr. George Conrad III

Contents

This book is dedicated to You. To the person who feels as though they've lost everything. To the person who feels unloveable. To the person who has scars from the past. To the person who feels broken. I see you. I hear you. You are treasured beyond measure. Your scars tell your story and make you strong. You are not broken. You deserve love. Don't stop looking for your melody.
~Tara

Prologue

VIKTOR'S GOODBYE

AFTER I SAY GOODBYE TO NATALIE, I TAKE A FEW minutes to pack my things and compose my thoughts before heading downstairs to meet with Alex. We need to talk. He deserves honesty about everything that's happened between me and Natalie, even if it changes things between us forever. Alex has been more than a boss—he's a friend. This conversation might cost me that friendship, but it has to be done.

When I get to the apartment, I find him and Misha having a late breakfast in the kitchen.

"Care to join us?" Alex asks, motioning to the spread. "Timur made enough for an army."

"No thanks. I only have a few minutes," I say, shifting my weight. "I was hoping we could talk."

Misha catches on and grabs his plate. "I have some work to do. I'll be in the office if you need me."

Once we're alone, I sit across from Alex. "You look better today." His color's returning, and he's already regaining strength.

"A good night's sleep and some food will do that." He studies me for a minute. "But I don't think you're here to tell me how good I look."

"No," I say, bracing myself. "I'm not."

Alex raises a hand to stop me. "Before you say anything. While Tommy was holding me, he showed me pictures and videos of you and Natalie together."

I go still, unsure how to respond. But he continues.

"What he didn't realize," he says slowly, "is that watching those videos brought me peace. It meant you were doing what I asked—making sure Natalie and Rose were safe and loved."

I'm stunned and at a loss for words. How do I tell him that being able to love his wife was the best time of my life?

Alex gives a slight nod. "I know how much you love her. I see it in the way you look at her. Part of me wonders if coming back into her life is even right. She loves you, Viktor, and Rose is bonded to you. Maybe they're better off without me."

"You're wrong," I say quietly. "Natalie does love me, but I'm her second choice. She'll never love me the way she does you. I want to keep her forever. God knows I do, but I can't. You're her heart. Her whole world."

My mind drifts back to the day we thought Alex died. The light in Natalie's eyes went out. I genuinely believe if it wasn't for being pregnant, she might've ended it then. Rose gave her a reason to keep going, but there was always an empty place in her heart. One I couldn't fill, no matter how much I loved her. That place always belonged to Alex. He's her destiny—her forever.

"I need to tell you everything that happened between Natalie and me," I say finally. "The parts you didn't see on Tommy's camera."

There's nothing easy about this. I stare down as I talk, unable to meet his gaze. Through it all, Alex remains silent. When I finish, he closes his eyes for a moment, absorbing it.

"I know that wasn't easy for you," he says, his voice rough. "It wasn't easy for me to hear. But I appreciate your honesty. That's why I chose you. I'll never forget what you've done for me."

I swallow hard, unsure of what to say.

"You needed to know everything before I leave."

He sits up, alert. "You're leaving?"

"I have to." I force myself to make eye contact, ready to accept whatever judgment he gives. "Alex, I'm in love with your wife. I can't and don't want to stop loving her."

"Does Natalie know?"

"Yes."

"And?"

"She begged me to stay. But there isn't room for both of us. She belongs with you."

"I see," Alex says quietly. "Words can't express my gratitude, Viktor. For the love you showed both of them. For... everything."

"There were days I hated you for asking it of us," I admit, "but I also want to thank you. I've never had a relationship like that. Loving her and having her love in return was an honor. She's an extraordinary woman. You're one hell of a lucky man."

"I'll never forget what you've done for us." He reaches out to shake my hand. "Please keep in touch."

I nod, gripping his hand. "Will do, boss," I say, though I know I won't. I need to make a clean break.

The elevator ride down to the underground parking is silent. When I step out, I spot Michael and the rest of the team waiting in the black SUV. I climb into the front passenger seat.

"You good?" Michael asks, glancing over.

I give a quick nod, afraid to speak. If I open my mouth, the dam holding back my emotions will break.

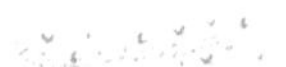

It's a long ride to the airport, and I spend it staring out the window, lost in thought. The landscape blurs past, but inside, my turmoil builds, each emotion fighting for space. The men in the back talk among themselves, but no one tries to draw me in.

When we arrive, Maxim's jet is on the tarmac, waiting for us to board. One by one, we climb out of the SUV, each man grabbing his luggage and heading toward the plane, eager to go home. But I remain by the vehicle, rooted in place, staring at the jet.

I'm at a crossroads, faced with the choice of boarding the plane and letting it take me to the other side of the world—away from the woman I love and the little girl who feels like my own. Or getting into the SUV, driving back to Natalie, and begging her to choose me.

"What's going on?" Michael's voice breaks through my thoughts. He stands beside me, watching.

I glance over. "Just debating my options."

"You know she's meant to be with him, Viktor. Your only option is to let her go and get on the plane. Set her free and give yourself permission to be free, too."

He claps a hand on my shoulder, then turns and heads toward the jet. His words linger, *set her free*. The truth hits hard. Natalie was never mine to keep. I close my eyes, take a deep breath, and steel myself. With one last look toward the horizon, I straighten my shoulders and walk to the plane.

Climbing the steps, I resist the urge to turn around, afraid that if I do, I won't have the strength to leave. Moments later, we're taxiing down the runway. The wheels lift from the ground, and New York City begins to fade beneath us.

As the plane ascends, the weight of my loss settles in. Tears slide down my face. I know I'm leaving a piece of my heart behind with a woman and a little girl who will always hold a part of me— no matter where I go.

Viktor

Set her free. I stare down at the diamond engagement ring I bought for Natalie, feeling a kind of hurt I never knew was possible. For ten months, I lived a life I'd never dared to dream of, and in a matter of minutes, it was gone.

I'm not a good man. Violence and death are woven into the fabric of my existence. Loving a woman is a weakness, But I would've kept her and Rose safe. I'd have given my life for them without a second thought.

What the hell kind of man am I that I wish Alex hadn't come back? That I could've had it all—the girl, a baby, a family of my own.

"Where are you running off to?" Dimitri's voice interrupts my thoughts as I make my way toward the back of the plane. "Being antisocial as usual?"

I can't deal with his shit right now. The best thing for both of us is for me to keep walking.

"Leave him alone," Sasha says, coming to my defense. "He's got a lot on his mind."

I don't wait to hear Dimitri's response before closing the door to the bedroom on Maxim's jet. I need to be alone to figure out how to piece together what's left of my life. To decide what my next step should be.

One of the problems awaiting me in Russia is Maxim. He's expecting us to meet at his house for our next assignment. But I can't go back there. Everything will remind me of her.

Taking out my phone, I book a commercial flight to Belgorod. Then, I send a message to my boss.

Me: I'm not coming back to work.

Maxim: Where are you going?

Me: Home.

I power off my phone, lean back, and close my eyes. Sleep drags me under, and in my dreams, Natalie's in my bed. My ring's on her finger—she's mine.

The wheels of the plane screech as we touch down on the runway. Thick clouds hide the moonlight, making it appear extra dark as we file off Max's jet. With their bags in hand, the team heads toward the waiting cars. But I walk in the opposite direction, toward the main terminal building.

"Viktor, where are you going?" Sasha calls out.

I don't answer, letting my silence speak for itself. Behind me, I hear the murmurs between the men. No one presses further, and no one follows.

Once again, I find myself alone.

Viktor

Compared to the flight from the states, the four-hour flight to Belgorod passes quickly. When I step outside the airport doors, I'm met by a shower and humid early morning air. The sun's just beginning to break through the remnants of night.

The taxi line stretches ahead, and I choose the nearest one. After tossing my bag onto the backseat, I slide in, give the driver my address, and settle in for the ride home.

Funny to think of it as home, I realize, almost surprised. This was the first apartment I bought while I was in the military, back in my early twenties. I rarely come back and barely ever think about it, yet somehow, it's always been here, waiting.

I've considered letting it go more than once, but somehow, I could never bring myself to do it. My gut told me I'd need it one day. Now, with nowhere else to go, it's all I have left.

"Are you from around here?" the cab driver asks, glancing at me in the rearview mirror.

"I grew up here."

"What brings you back?"

"A woman," I answer, not elaborating.

He raises an eyebrow. "Usually, when a man comes back for a woman, he looks happier than you are right now."

"I'm not coming back for her," I say flatly. "We aren't together anymore."

His face softens. "I'm very sorry."

"So am I," I reply quietly, turning to watch the city pass by, feeling the familiar ache set in.

I'm thankful when the cab comes to a stop in front of my apartment building. Inside my date, a bottle of premium Russian liquor waits.

"Thanks for the ride," I say, handing the driver a stack of rubles and reaching for the door.

The driver turns slightly in his seat. *"Inagda shto-ka kharosheye ne sluchayesta, shtoby maglo sluchitsa shto-ta luchsheye."*

"Khoroshego dnya," I respond, ignoring the sting of his words. Nothing will *"fall together"* for me. Natalie was my one shot at love. I won't make that mistake again.

The thought lingers as I unlock the door. Stepping inside, I'm met with a strange sense of unfamiliarity.

When I bought this place, I'd hoped my *babusya* would move here so I could care for her. It would've made things easier, but she refused to leave her small Ukranian village. Instead, I made the hour-long trip every week, bringing her supplies and spending time with her.

I toss my bag onto the counter and head to the fridge. It's fully stocked, just as I asked. I pay Zoya, my housekeeper, well to keep the place ready—an odd request, maybe, since no one lives here.

While I was on the flight from New York, I'd texted her to stock up, making sure she didn't forget the vodka. I pull out the bottle first, skip the glass, and drink straight from it, desperately trying to numb the ache in my heart.

Viktor

WARMTH FLOWS THROUGH MY VEINS AS THE VODKA begins to work its way through my system. I close my eyes, and my mind drifts back in time.

My mother was a student at the Bolshoi Ballet Academy, one of the most prestigious ballet academies in Russia. Her dream was to become a premier dancer. At seventeen, she met my father, a *Serzhánt* in the Soviet army, three years older than her. Typically, the academy's students weren't allowed to date. However, because of his position, he received special permission to court her while she was still a student.

Six months after they met, she became pregnant and was kicked out of the academy. Her dreams of dancing professionally were over. In the 1980s, an unwed mother faced harsh judgment, so they married quickly. Not long after, Papa retired from the military, and they moved to his hometown—Belgorod.

My parents adored each other. One of my fondest memories is of them dancing together in the kitchen. Papa would come home from work and go straight to Mama. He'd take her in his arms and start humming a tune. She'd light up as he spun her around, completely lost in each other.

They were incredible parents. Mama gave me all her attention, and Papa taught me how to be a man. I wanted to be just like him. Their only sadness was not being able to give me a sibling. They wanted a second child, but it never happened.

And then, their lives were cut short.

It was late December. Papa had planned a special trip to Moscow to take Mama to see The Nutcracker. I was thirteen, practically an adult in my eyes, and begged to stay home alone. But Mama insisted I was too young to be left alone for an entire weekend. Instead, *Babusya* came to stay with me.

"I'm going to miss you, Vitya," Mama said, pressing a tearful kiss to my forehead.

"Olena, he's no longer a child. He'll be fine," Papa assured her, placing a comforting arm around her shoulders.

"He'll always be my baby, Nikita," she'd replied, wiping her eyes. Then they turned to me.

"Mind your grandmother," Papa reminded me.

"Yes, sir."

"We'll see you in a few days."

I watched as Papa helped Mama into the car and loaded their luggage. Mama waved goodbye as they drove off.

Babusya and I spent the weekend preparing for Christmas. We baked dozens of *Pryaniki*, Ukaranian spice cookies, and got to work on their Christmas gift. She didn't believe in store-bought presents, saying a handmade gift had more value. So, we spent hours painting a set of hand-carved *Matryoshka* dolls that a village artisan had made for us. It was a painstaking process, but by the end of the weekend, they were perfect.

The night they were supposed to come home, I was in my room, finishing the wrapping. A knock on the door interrupted me. I heard the low murmur of voices followed by a blood-curdling scream. I rushed into the hallway to find *Babusya* on her knees, wailing, while a uniformed officer stood in the doorway.

"What's going on?" I demanded, my protective instincts kicking in.

The officer turned to me. "Are you Viktor Volkov?"

"Yes."

"I'm very sorry to inform you that your parents were killed in a car accident earlier this evening."

For a moment, I could only stare, convinced there had been a mistake. My parents couldn't be dead. They were on their way home to me. But the look on the officer's face shattered that hope.

Putting on a brave face, I helped my grief-stricken grandmother up from the floor and gently guided her to a chair. The officer explained there was a heavy snow squall. Visibility dropped quickly, and the roads because slick. An oncoming car had been speeding when they lost control and crossed into my parents' lane. They were hit head-on. The emergency responders said they died upon impact.

At thirteen, I became an orphan.

After the officer left, *Babusya* began preparing the house for the mourning period. Because my parents' death was sudden and tragic, a *bad death*, she followed tradition. She covered each mirror with black cloth and stopped all the clocks.

"Why are you doing this, Babusya?" I asked, confused by her actions.

"Mirrors are gateways to the land of the dead," she said quietly. *"The first person to see their reflection will be the next to die."*

"Why stop the clocks? How will we know the time?"

"Vitya, when a person dies suddenly, their soul lingers on earth for forty days," she explained patiently. *"Because your parents' death was an accident, they will remain longer. By stopping the clocks, we help them transition to the afterlife quicker."*

Later that day, mourners began arriving, bringing food and mementos to place in their caskets. They shared stories of my parents, memories I tried to listen to, but I was numb. I kept hoping to wake up from this nightmare. I was still expecting them to walk through the door.

But they never did.

Instead, we packed my belongings, and I said goodbye to my

friends and the life I'd known. *Babuysa* took me to live in her small village. That's when I took her surname, Dobrow.

A few years later, another upheaval came—the fall of the Soviet Union. The village of *Bobrivka* was no longer part of Russia. We were now citizens of Ukraine, an independent country. I lived with her until I turned eighteen and finished school. After that, I enlisted in the Ukrainian army as a conscript.

That's when I met Dimitri. He had a similar story to mine. Originally from St. Petersburg, his father, a soldier in the Soviet Union, died during the battles that ended communism. Afterward, Dimitri's mother moved them to her home, which was now part of Ukraine.

We spent hours reminiscing about our childhoods in Russia. As kids, communism was an abstract concept. All we knew was that we had our families and friends. But then, we lost the people we loved, and our worlds were turned upside down.

Dimitri had family in Russia and planned to return to St. Petersburg after his service. "You should come with me," he urged. "My uncle promised me a job. We'll make more money than we could ever dream of."

And so we went.

I had no idea who Dimitri's uncle was or how my life would forever be changed after meeting Maxim Solonik. The skills we learned in the military translated well, and soon, we were making more money than any totally legal job could ever pay.

My first priority was sending money to *Babusya* to make sure she had everything she needed. She resisted, claiming she didn't need so much, and I suspected she gave most of it away. But I kept sending it anyway.

Then, I bought this apartment.

Which brings me right back to the present and why I'm drinking.

Natalie—the woman I'm in love with. The woman I had to give back to her husband. With each pull from the bottle, I try to forget the past and numb the pain of losing her.

Viktor

THE BRIGHT MORNING SUN STREAMING THROUGH THE window wakes me. My head throbs, and I realize I'm lying on the floor, though I don't know why—until I spot the empty vodka bottles beside me. Then it all comes rushing back.

Slowly, I stand, steadying myself as the room spins. I press a hand against the wall for balance and pull the heavy curtains closed, blocking the blinding sunlight that only worsens my headache. Once the room is dark again, I make my way to the bathroom, hoping to find something to dull the pounding in my head.

In the medicine cabinet, I find a bottle of Calpol. I pour three tablets into my hand and head back to the kitchen to find something to drink. I consider washing them down with more vodka. To spend another day in an alcohol-induced haze but settle for water instead.

After swallowing the pills, I step into a hot shower, letting the steam wash away the remnants of last night. I have something important to do today, and I need to be sober for it. Once I'm dressed and my headache has faded to a dull throb, I grab a quick bite to eat.

With my keys in hand, I head down to the parking garage and

uncover my Harley. I bought her a few years back in the States and had her shipped here, though it's been far too long since I've ridden. The engine rumbles beneath me as I start her up, a low growl that reverberates through my bones. Then, I pull out of the garage and ride through the city.

When I reach the other side of town, I stop at a florist and buy eight of their finest yellow roses. The steady thud of my boots echoes along the brick path to the cemetery's entrance. When I reach the tall black wrought iron gate, I pause, almost losing my nerve. It would be easier to turn around, get back on my bike, and go home—like I've done so many times over the past fourteen years.

But not today. It's time to face my past. I pull open the gate and step inside.

Although I haven't been here since the day my parents were buried, I remember exactly where they lie entombed in the earth. It's a somber walk along the stone path that weaves through rows of headstones marking the resting places of others' loved ones.

I stop in front of their memorial—*Nikita Volkov and Olena Volkova*. Like so many others here, their faces are etched into the stone, digitally frozen in time. I stare at them, trying to recall the details of their faces and the sound of their voices. It's been so long. The realization that I can't picture them as clearly as I used to hits me hard, and I sink down onto the grass.

"Mama, I miss you so much." My voice is barely a whisper. "I fell in love with a woman. Her name's Natalie. You and she would've gotten along so well." I reach out and trace Mama's photo with my finger. "She has a baby girl, Rose. The baby isn't mine, but I was there when she was born. I loved her and learned how to take care of her. I know you would've loved both of them."

"I was going to marry her. But it was complicated. Almost a year after we were told her husband died in a tragic accident, we found out he was alive. And just like that, I lost everything." I stop to wipe away the tears that are falling freely now.

I'm a man. I shouldn't be crying, especially not in public. "I should've known better. I don't deserve someone as wonderful as Natalie. I don't deserve any woman. And I sure as hell don't deserve to be any child's father."

For so many years, I avoided facing my loss. I refused to face the fact that my parents were gone. That's why I took *Babusya's* last name. I wanted to fit in with my friends and have a *normal* family like everyone else. Whenever a schoolmate asked, I'd pretend that she was my mother. She never corrected me, letting me live in my made-up world. Now, I'm ashamed that I tried to erase my real parents from my life.

But as much as I miss them, there's a part of me that's relieved they're not here to see who I've become. Papa would never approve of the choices I've made, and Mama would be heartbroken that I'll never marry or give her grandchildren. As much as I miss them, their deaths spared them the disappointment of seeing the man I've become.

"Please forgive me, Papa," I murmur, staring at his image. "You were my hero. The man I wanted to grow up to be. I wish I could promise to change, to be someone you'd be proud of. But I can't walk away from the life I've built."

If only I knew when they left that night that it would be our final goodbye. I would have told them I loved them, held on a little longer.

I close my eyes, letting the silence envelop me as if hoping to hear their voices one last time. Praying for their forgiveness.

Finally, I lay the eight yellow roses, Mama's favorite, on their grave. "I love you both."

Viktor

"I'll be out of touch for a while," I say, throwing my belongings into my bag as I speak.

"Where will you be?" Maxim asks.

"There's something I need to take care of. Someone I need to see."

"How long will you be gone?"

"I'll be in touch when I can." I end the call without waiting for his response.

With my bag slung over one shoulder, I head out, ready for the road ahead.

The rumble of my motorcycle draws attention as I pull into the tiny village of *Bobrivka*. Children stop to point and giggle, curious about the loud machine. No one here owns a car, let alone a motorcycle. I slow down, maneuvering carefully along the rough paths, until I see the familiar clay house with its thatched roof.

As I near, the wooden door creaks open, and a woman in a brightly colored *fuska* peers out. Her back is slightly hunched, and she leans on a cane. She looks much older than the last time I saw her. Her blue eyes, so much like my own, light up with recognition as I stop in front of her.

"Viktor, is it really you?"

"It's me, *Babusya*."

"*Miy onuk* has come home." She opens her arms, and I wrap her frail frame in a hug as she begins to cry.

"*Tak, Babusya.* I'm home."

Gently, I take her arm and lead her inside, wanting privacy for our reunion. Nothing in her modest home has changed. She's always lived a simple existence. The living room still has just a tattered sofa draped with a handmade blanket and a matching chair. I can almost picture *Dido* sitting there, smoking his pipe. Her kitchen is old-fashioned—traditional, she calls it, with an old wood stove and shelves lined with jars of preserved food. It's nothing like the modern houses I've become used to, but it's comfortable—it's home.

Like the other homes in the village, hers has no modern wiring or plumbing. A few years back, despite her protests, I gave her a cell phone and installed a small solar generator. I wanted to add some modern wiring to make life easier, but she refused. After many arguments, she relented and agreed to keep the generator solely to charge her cell phone—the one she never leaves turned on.

"Where is your love?" she asks softly.

I look away, feeling a familiar ache.

"*Vitya?* Why do you look so sad?"

"She's gone," I say, and we sit together on the sofa as I try to explain. Her eyes fill with compassion as she listens, and once again, I find myself struggling to hold back tears. This raw emotion is foreign and uncomfortable.

"I'm so sorry, my dear boy," she says, squeezing my hand. "You deserve happiness."

"No, *Babusya*. I don't."

She tuts, patting my hand firmly. "There will be no more talk like that. You are Viktor Dobrow, my beloved grandson who deserves everything good in this life." She offers a gentle smile. "Now, come with me. I need to bring in the laundry." She moves to stand, but her legs falter.

I rush to catch her, helping her settle back onto the sofa. "Are you okay?"

She reaches into her pocket, pulling out a small glass bottle. Shaking out a pill, she slips it under her tongue.

"What's that for?" I ask, alarmed.

"It's nothing."

"It's not nothing. Tell me, please."

With a sigh, she looks at me sadly. "I'm dying, *Vitya*."

The words hit like a punch to the gut, leaving me breathless. Dying? That can't be true. She's all I have left.

"What do you mean?" I ask, struggling to keep my voice steady.

"My heart is old and tired."

"I'll take you to a doctor." I pull out my phone, ready to call Maxim and find her the best care.

But she places her hand over mine, stopping me. "I've already seen one."

"Then I'll find you a better one."

"There's too much damage." She shakes her head. "I don't have much time left."

My grandmother explains that she had a major heart attack several months ago. Fortunately, she'd been visiting a neighbor, who called the village doctor. He stabilized her long enough to get her to a bigger hospital in Kharkiv.

"They poked and prodded at me for days," she says. "The tests showed there was much damage to my heart."

"There are surgeries, medications—"

She holds up a hand. "I'm an old woman, *Vitya*. Too old for surgery."

"Then come back to Belgorod with me," I urge, desperation edging my voice. "I'll hire a nurse. We'll find the best doctors."

"No," she says firmly, standing with difficulty. "I will not spend my remaining days in a strange place surrounded by doctors who treat me like a lab experiment. I belong here."

"*Babusya*, please—"

"There will be no argument, *onuk*. My decision is final."

Now isn't the time to push, so I try another approach. "Why didn't you call me? I would've come to take care of you." Guilt gnaws at me. She's my responsibility, and I've failed her.

"I have not been alone. Yelyzaveta comes every day to help me." She smiles, but I see the sadness behind it. "But not of that matters because you're here now."

Yelyzaveta. I haven't thought of her in years. Growing up, she was a year younger than me. Although western dating wasn't something practiced in the village, she and I spent all our free time together. Everyone in the village assumed we'd marry someday. But that was a long time ago. She's probably married now, with children of her own.

I follow *Babusya* outside to the clothesline, where she takes down her laundry, dropping it into the woven basket at her feet.

"Here, let me." I step in front of her, taking over.

"I'm perfectly capable of handling my own laundry," she protests, hands on her hips.

"As am I."

She mutters, "*Vpertyy khlopchyk.*"

"I learned to be stubborn from the best." I grin, carrying the basket back inside as she follows, grumbling under her breath.

"Put it on the table," she instructs, waving a hand, "then go get settled in your room. I'll fold it while I cook dinner." I open my mouth to argue, but she holds up a finger. "Do not argue with an old woman."

Shaking my head, I grab my bag and open the wooden door to what was once my bedroom. Everything looks the same. Untouched as if it were preserved in a time capsule. Handmade blue curtains hang over the window, faded with age. The bed is made with white sheets and the patchwork quilt *Babusya* crafted from pieces of my parents' clothing, so I'd always have them close. As a child, I never appreciated it, but now the familiarity brings a sense of peace. I sit on the edge of the bed, letting memories wash over me, before unpacking what few belongings I brought.

When I return to the kitchen, my grandmother is at the counter, rolling cabbage leaves around a meat mixture. I recognize it instantly—*holubtsi*, a favorite dish of mine from childhood.

"Did you grow the cabbage?" I ask, settling into a chair.

"Of course," she replies with a smile. "Now sit and rest. Dinner will be ready soon."

Her hands move deftly, and I watch in silence, grateful to be back in this small, familiar world, even if only for a little while.

Viktor

VIKTOR

Settling back into the village and returning to a simpler way of life has been an adjustment. There's no television or internet here, no rush to get from one place to another. Besides my cell phone, I'm fully unplugged from the digital world. Part of me finds comfort in the isolation, while another part craves my usual pace.

I've sent Babusya to rest while I rake out the chicken coop and gather the eggs. She works far too hard for her age.

"I can get those," a feminine voice says behind me.

"It's already done."

Carrying a bowl full of eggs, I step out of the hens' enclosure and find Yelyzaveta waiting. The beautiful woman standing in front of me is the grown-up version of the fair-skinned, hazel-eyed girl I once knew.

"I heard you were home," she says softly. "How is Anoushka today?"

"She's well." I start toward the house. "Babusya told me you come by daily to check on her, yet I haven't seen you in the two weeks I've been here."

"Mama thought you might want time alone with her. But I can start coming by if you'd like."

As much as I want to care for *Babusya* myself, there are things she needs help with that aren't appropriate for me to handle.

"I would appreciate that."

"I can look in on her now if you'd like."

"She's napping at the moment."

Veta's eyes brighten. "Would you take a walk with me? Like we used to?"

I set the eggs by the door. "As long as we're not too long. I don't like leaving *Babusya* alone for extended periods."

We stroll down the main path through the village. "It's surprising how little things have changed here."

She gives a small laugh. "What did you expect?"

"I thought maybe the younger generation would've brought in some modern technology—even basic things, like running water and electricity."

Veta shakes her head, smiling. "I don't think that'll ever happen."

We walk quietly until we reach the small lake on the edge of the village. Wildflowers line the bank, and frogs croak among the lily pads. I recall our childhood, how we'd race through our chores to come here on hot days, eager to jump into the cool water.

"Anoushka told me you met someone. Is it serious?"

"It was. But we're not together anymore."

"I'm sorry to hear that."

"What about you? Are you married?"

"No." Her reply is almost shy.

I look at her, surprised. "When we were kids, you always talked about marrying and having children."

She tucks a strand of honey-colored hair behind her ear. "I've had proposals. But I turned them down."

"Why?"

Veta hesitates, meeting my gaze. "Because none of them came from the man I'm in love with."

The intensity in her eyes is unmistakable. Before I can respond, an older man approaches.

"You must be Viktor." He extends his hand.

"And you are?"

"Volodymyr. I'm the village doctor."

I shake his hand. "Good to meet you. I've been wanting to discuss treatment options for my grandmother."

He glances between Yelyzeveta and me. "I can stop by the house later if that's more convenient."

"I'd prefer to talk now if you have the time. Every minute we delay feels like wasted time. I'm afraid if we don't do something soon, *Babusya* will run out of tomorrows."

Veta places a gentle hand on my arm. "I'll check on Anoushka before heading home."

"Thank you. I'll see you tomorrow."

Once she leaves, the doctor watches her go and turns back to me. "Old friends?" he asks, eyebrows raised.

"Yes, just old friends," I clarify, brushing off his curiosity.

He nods. "Understood."

"I want a more aggressive approach to my grandmother's treatment. Just managing her symptoms here in the village isn't enough. I want to take her back to Belgorod with me."

Volodymyr sighs. "Anoushka's a very stubborn woman. I doubt you'll have much success with that."

As we talk, he explains more about her health. "The only reason I managed to get her to Kharkiv was because she was unconscious most of the way. Once she stabilized, she was back to her usual self." He chuckles but soon grows serious. "Your grandmother's lucky to be alive, Viktor. The tests revealed significant heart damage. It took some coaxing, but she eventually admitted to shortness of breath and chest pain that she'd been experiencing for months."

Frustration builds as I listen. "I can get her the best doctors. Surely, they can—"

He shakes his head. "There's nothing more anyone can do.

Even if the damage were fixable, she isn't strong enough for surgery. All we can do now is manage the symptoms and keep her comfortable."

I clench my jaw, barely containing my frustration. "Why wasn't I called sooner? She has my number on the cell phone I gave her."

"We tried. She refused to let anyone contact you."

"I don't care—"

"Viktor." Volodymyr's voice is firm but understanding. "I know you want to help, but she's my patient, and I must respect *her* wishes. I'll do everything I can to ensure she's comfortable and that when her time comes, she'll pass with dignity."

I hear his words, but I can't accept them. He may be a capable doctor, but he doesn't understand what's possible beyond this village. My connections can get the best doctors in the world. Until I've exhausted every option, I refuse to believe nothing can be done.

"I need to get back to her."

He nods, sympathetic. "I'll walk with you. She's on my list of patients to see today."

Viktor

AUTUMN IS RAPIDLY COMING TO A CLOSE. THE LAST warm days are giving way to cooler air, a sure sign that winter is on its way. Unfortunately, as the seasons shift, so does *Babusya*. Every day, she grows weaker, her breathing more labored. She tries to hide it, but I see the strain.

For the past hour, I've been in my room staring at my phone with Maxim's contact pulled up. The doctor urged me to respect her wishes rather than spend our time fighting, but how can I sit by and watch her die when I have the resources to help?

"Are you ready to go?" *Babusya* calls from the kitchen.

"I'll be right there," I respond, tucking the phone away.

For weeks now, we've been canning vegetables from her garden. The village has a way of life that emphasizes family and community. Everyone contributes to their household and shares with neighbors. It's how they've not only survived but thrived for generations.

The elderly, like my grandmother, don't need to keep working, but she insists. It's part of her. I can't imagine her doing anything else as long as she's breathing.

Last night, after we finished the last of the work, I loaded the jars onto her wagon in preparation for today's deliveries. The decision on whether or not to call Max will have to wait a little longer. But I know I can't put it off much past today.

"You're finally ready," she says when I come out of my room.

"Sorry," I say, leaning down to kiss her cheek. "Be sure to put your coat on. It's chilly."

"My boy is trying to be the parent," she teases, though she grabs her coat with a small smile.

"No. I care about you and don't want you getting sick."

She pats my cheek. "You're a good man, *Vitya*."

Ignoring her words, I grip the wagon's handle. "Let's go."

Together, we walk through the village, dropping off food at each home. At every stop, her neighbors invite us in to sit and reminisce. This village is all they know. Their lives are woven together. They may not be connected by blood, but that doesn't make them any less of a family.

While they talk, I watch *Babusya*. Her happiness radiates with each home we enter. Understandably, she doesn't want to leave, but that doesn't make her decision right. Leaving wouldn't be forever—just long enough for her to get the care she needs.

When we step outside one of the homes, I take her arm. "You look tired, *Babusya*. Let's go home."

"We have one more stop."

"I'll do it tomorrow."

"No, we will go now," she insists.

I give in and help her to the last house—Yelyzeveta's family home.

The door opens before we even knock, and Veta's mother greets us. "Anoushka, you look well today. Please, come in." She turns to me with a smile. "Viktor, it's wonderful to have you back."

"Thank you, Ksenia." I lean in to kiss her on both cheeks.

"I just put tea on. Will you stay for a cup?"

"Maybe next—"

"Of course we will," *Babusya* interjects, cutting me off with a grin.

"Veta," Ksenia calls, "please set out two more cups."

"Who's—" Veta appears around the corner and freezes when she sees me. It only takes her a second to recover. She turns to my grandmother with a smile. "Anoushka, it's so good to see you out. And you too, Viktor."

The afternoon stretches on as we share tea and listen to Ksenia and *Babusya* recount stories from our childhood. They laugh about old pranks and retell memories I'd nearly forgotten.

"Yuri and I always thought Yelyzeveta and Viktor would end up married one day," Ksenia says with a twinkle in her eye.

"As did I," *Babusya* adds, not missing a beat.

Glancing at Veta, I notice a hint of sadness in her eyes. Did she believe it, too? I feel everyone's eyes on me as if they're expecting a response. A declaration of love. But there's nothing to offer.

"Mama, don't put Viktor on the spot," Veta murmurs, looking away. "That was a long time ago."

"It was, but love can span distance and time. You'll soon discover that," *Babusya* says with a knowing smile.

"We should start for home," I say, steering the conversation away.

"Why don't you stay for dinner?" Ksenia suggests.

Staying is the last thing I want, but I defer to my grandmother.

"Thank you for the invitation," she replies, "but I'm getting tired. Perhaps another time?"

"Of course. Yelyzeveta will let me know when you're up to it."

We say our goodbyes and begin the slow walk home at a pace much slower than before.

"I'm so glad you came home, dear boy," *Babusya* says between labored breaths.

"I still wish you'd called sooner."

"You're here now."

"But we could've had more time," I murmur.

More time. It seems that's become a theme echoing through my life. Always longing for more time with the people I love.

My parents. Natalie and Rose.

And now, these precious days with *Babusya*.

I can almost hear the clock ticking, each second reminding me that our time together is slipping away.

Maxim

IRINA AND I ARE AT JELENA'S HOPE. ALTHOUGH AMELIA is progressing well, she continues to attend therapy sessions once a week. Irina is visiting a few of our guests who are preparing to transition into community housing. I'm using the time to check on the construction team. We are expanding the building to accommodate more recovered persons. Most places would see an expansion as a success—yet here, it is a grim reminder of the evil that exists.

Our growth reflects the relentless spread of human trafficking. Some days, it feels as if dismantling one ring only gives rise to three more. It is discouraging, but it is a fight I will not give up. As long as I am breathing, I will continue to hunt these animals and take them down.

The construction foreman gives me a progress update when my phone vibrates in my pocket. Viktor's name appears on the screen. "Excuse me," I tell the foreman. "I need to take this." Walking a few steps away, I answer the call. "Viktor?"

"Hi," he says quietly.

I hesitate, noting the unusual tone in his voice. "How are things going there?"

"Not well," he replies, his voice tinged with sorrow. Viktor rarely calls unless it's about work, and I can tell this is different. "My grandmother is dying."

His words catch me off guard.

"She won't let me help her. What do I do, Max? I can't lose her. Not now."

Viktor is not a boy, but the vulnerability in his voice sounds almost childlike. He has endured more loss than most in his thirty-two years, and even now, while he is home to recover from losing Natalie, he is facing another tragedy.

"Bring her here," I suggest. "I will arrange for the best doctors."

"I've tried," he says, sounding defeated. "She refuses to leave. Won't even let me bring anyone in. She's content to die."

"Anoushka has always been strong-willed," I say gently. "She was not afraid to challenge me head-on when you first came to work for me." I chuckle at the memory. "She raised you to be the man you are, Viktor. Now, it is your turn to care for her in the way she wishes."

"But I have the means to get—"

"No," I interrupt. "You must honor her wishes as she faces the end of her life. This will no doubt be the hardest job you have ever done."

He is quiet, then murmurs, "I don't know if I can do this, Max."

"You will find the strength." I pause, then add, "Alexander called, asking about you."

I had not planned on mentioning it, but maybe knowing someone cares will encourage him. Viktor and Alexander share a deep, if not complex, bond. I hope this knowledge prompts him to reach out.

"What did you tell him?"

"That you went home for some time off. And you are doing well."

"Does he know where I am?"

"No."

"Thank you. I need this distance right now."

"I understand you need the space, but think about calling him. Alexander values your friendship."

"I'm probably the last person Alex wants to hear from."

"Do not shut him out, Viktor. Just consider it."

"Yeah."

I do not press further. He needs his friends now more than ever, but pushing him might only drive him further away. "If there is anything you need, do not hesitate to call me."

We say our goodbyes, and I prepare to go in search of Irina. But when I turn around, she is already there.

"I didn't want to interrupt," she says softly.

"Thank you, *vozlyublenny*." I kiss her cheek. "It was Viktor. He is struggling."

She frowns in concern. "Where is he?"

"With Anoushka. It will be some time before he will be ready to return." I glance around. "Is Amelia ready?"

"Yes, she's waiting for us in the lobby."

"Let us get our girl and go home."

My heart is heavy, carrying the weight of Viktor's pain. I understand too well what it is to watch someone you love slip away, unable to stop it. My only hope is that he has someone by his side. But I know no one can spare him from the pain he will face shortly.

It is a road he must traverse alone.

Viktor

Drawn to the water, I walk to the stream at the edge of the village before placing the call. Talking to Max has brought up memories I haven't revisited in years—especially the day I left this place behind.

Babusya wasn't pleased when I told her I was going to Russia for work. My excitement was genuine as I shared a carefully crafted story about Maxim's involvement in clean energy and how I'd be working with him in this up-and-coming field.

But *Babusya* didn't buy my story for a second.

"Vitya, you know nothing about this energy business," she said, eyeing me shrewdly. "I may be an old lady, but I'm not dumb. You're up to no good." She wagged a finger at me, unimpressed.

I chuckle now, remembering how she'd planted herself in front of the door, hands on her hips, refusing to let me pass. I politely asked her to move, but she refused, glaring at me. I had to lift her up and physically move her to get out the door.

My work is dangerous, but Maxim has been very good to me. He's the closest thing to a father I've had in years. Hearing his voice was comforting, even though I didn't like his advice. He's right, though. I can't change what's happening—my grandmother is dying. There's no stopping it.

What really surprised me was hearing that Alex had asked about me. He graciously accepted my apology, but I figured he'd be relieved I was out of his and Natalie's lives. Still, a part of me misses our friendship.

The thought pulls me back to a place I'd been trying to avoid. I open the gallery app on my phone, scrolling through pictures of happier times. Selfies with Natalie. Stolen moments of Natalie with Rose, tender interactions she didn't know I was capturing at the time. Videos of baby Rose giggling and calling for *Friker*.

Natalie.

God, I miss her so much it physically hurts. During the day, the smallest thing, a scent or a sound, triggers memories of her. At night, she fills my dreams. I wake up reaching out, but she's no longer curled up next to me. Everything in me wants to call her to hear her voice. But I can't. She's no longer mine. Natalie is with Alex, where she was always meant to be.

Swallowing the memories back down, I close the photos and tuck the phone away. There are other matters that need my attention now.

When I return to the house, *Babusya* is sitting outside. Her cheeks are grayish, and her lips have a faint blue tint. Every day, her heart fails her a little more. But her cyan-blue eyes still light up when she sees me. I'm thankful I came home when I did. That I have these last precious days with her.

"Why are you out here?" I ask, reaching for her arm. "It's too chilly. You'll catch a cold."

She swats my hand away, scowling. "I asked Veta to bring me out," she says, pausing to catch her breath. "I wanted fresh air."

"Where's Veta?" My voice hardens. She should know better than to leave her alone in this cold.

"I sent her home."

"You know I don't like you being alone."

She waves me off, and I take a deep breath, steadying myself.

"I wanted to talk to you alone," she says firmly.

I sit down beside her in a rickety wooden chair. "All right, what is it?"

"You. And Yelyzeveta." She turns to face me. "You two were always meant to be together. Neither of you has married. Now, after all these years, fate has brought you back together."

"*Babusya*," I sigh, unamused by her matchmaking.

"She's a good woman and will make a fine wife. You can marry and have a family. This house will be yours. You can build a life here."

"How do I even know she wants that?"

"Oh, Vitya, my boy," she says, patting my arm. "Yelyzeveta has waited for you to return. She always believed you'd come back someday."

Waited for me? Why would she do that?

"You've been invited to dinner this evening as part of your courtship," she announces as if it's settled.

"I'm not leaving you alone," I reply, crossing my arms.

"Ksenia will be along to sit with me."

"I'd rather stay here with you." I stand. "Let me make you something to eat."

"No. I'm not hungry."

She's barely eaten anything for days now.

"You need to eat, *Babusya*. To keep up your strength."

She shakes her head, smiling faintly. "I won't be here much longer."

"Don't say that," I murmur.

Her hand rests on my arm, and I cover it with my own. Her skin is thin and fragile, cold to the touch. As if her body is betraying her and breaking down.

"I'm grateful for each day I wake," she says quietly, "but I do not fear death."

Death.

It's not death itself I fear—I've stared it down countless times. Confronted it. Brought it to many people. It's living in the silence it leaves behind. It's wanting to touch and talk to loved ones who are no longer here.

It's being alone.

We sit there, her hand in mine, watching her neighbors go about their daily lives. Women pull laundry off clotheslines while young children toddle at their feet. Older children run in the streets, laughing and playing. The men work in the fields, preparing for winter. Life in this village has stayed the same, as though they live in a time capsule.

And then, another realization settles over me. When *Babusya* passes, life here will go on—without her. Sure, there will be a mourning period, but afterward, people will return to their routines. She'll become a memory, just another part of the past. The thought is a sobering reminder of how quickly life moves forward.

Viktor

AFTER GETTING MY GRANDMOTHER IN THE HOUSE, I make a cup of tea to warm her up. Then, I head to my room to change for dinner. A date is the last thing I want tonight, but I won't disrespect *Babusya* or Yelyzeveta by refusing.

My options are limited since I packed light—jeans and a T-shirt will have to do. I glance in the small mirror atop the dresser. It's been years since I've let my hair grow out, and my reflection feels oddly unfamiliar. I run a hand through the blond strands and shrug. Good enough. Grabbing my jacket off the bed, I return to the main room.

Ksenia is already here. She's sitting on the sofa with my grandmother. The comforting smell of soup fills the house, and I notice a pot simmering on the stove. Ksenia must have brought dinner. Hopefully, she can coax my grandmother to eat.

"You look very handsome this evening, *Vitya*," Ksenia remarks with a warm smile.

"Thank you, ma'am." I walk over to *Babusya*. "Please, try to eat something. I won't be late."

She waves me off with a smile, exchanging a conspiratorial look with Ksenia. "Take your time. Ksenia will keep me company."

I shake my head, bending down to kiss her cheek. "All right. I'll see you later."

"Enjoy yourself, Viktor," she says softly.

I nod, heading out the door. The sun dips below the horizon, casting a warm glow over the quiet village as I make my way to Veta's house. The streets are empty. Everyone has gone inside for dinner. Here, without electricity, the people follow the sun's rhythms—early to bed, early to rise.

When I reach her house, I knock. After a moment, the door opens, and Veta greets me.

"I'm glad you came," she says, stepping aside. "Please, come in."

"Thanks for the invitation," I reply, following her inside.

She leads me to the kitchen, where the table is set for two. The soft glow from the oil lamp casts a cozy light over the room, giving it a surprisingly intimate feel. It reminds me of the Valentine's Day dinner I once planned for Natalie—a bittersweet memory. I force myself to put that aside and try to remain in the present moment.

"You're a little early," Veta says with a small laugh. "Dinner won't be ready for a few more minutes."

"Can I help with anything?" I offer.

She chuckles softly. "No. You sit and relax."

I forget how old-fashioned the expectations are here. There have always been traditional views of men's and women's roles. Even though I'm more than capable of helping, she pulls out a chair, waiting for me to sit.

Veta's modest blue dress flutters as she moves gracefully around the kitchen. Several loose curls frame her face. Every now and then, she reaches up, checking the pins in her hair. Soon, she begins bringing dishes to the table. She reaches behind her to untie her apron, but as hard as she tries, it doesn't come undone.

"It seems I've knotted it," she says, glancing over her shoulder. "Could you help?"

My hands shake as I work to untie the strings. Natalie used to wear an apron, too, one with a ridiculous pumpkin pattern. She'd always wrap the strings around her waist and tie them in front to avoid this very issue.

"There, I got it," I say, stepping back.

"Thank you." She sets the apron aside and joins me at the table.

Dinner is delicious, full of fresh ingredients and flavors that only a home-cooked meal can offer. Conversation flows effortlessly between us. I find myself smiling and laughing more than I expected.

"What are your plans now that you're back?" she asks, glancing at me curiously.

"I haven't really thought about it," I admit. "Right now, I'm focused on taking care of *Babusya*."

"She hasn't stopped smiling since you came home."

Home.

Once upon a time, this place was my home. Compared to the rush of New York City, life here is slower, simpler—untouched by the chaos of the modern world. But can I really see myself staying here permanently?

"Viktor." Veta waves her hand in front of my face, pulling me back. "You seemed like you were somewhere else."

"Sorry," I murmur and stand up. "Let me help you clear the table."

"This is woman's work," she says, carrying the dishes to the sink. "Would you like something to drink?"

"No, thank you." I walk to the window, gazing into the darkness. "Veta, would you ever consider leaving the village?"

She turns and leans against the wooden countertop. "That's an odd question. Why do you ask?"

"I'm just curious."

"For the right man, I'd go anywhere," she says, moving closer. "But I'd want to come back someday. I love it here and want to raise my children in this village."

We linger in silence, caught in a moment that stretches

between us. Then, she rises onto her toes and kisses me. I slide my hands into her hair, loosening it from its pins, then grip the back of her neck, deepening the kiss.

"Viktor, stop." Her hands press against my chest, creating space between us.

I let go immediately, taking a step back as I catch my breath.

"What was that?" she asks as she quickly pins her hair back up.

"It was a kiss," I say, struggling to hide my confusion. She kissed me first. But when I closed my eyes, it wasn't Veta whose lips were kissing mine. It was Natalie's hair threaded through my fingers. "Isn't that what you wanted?" I ask, confused.

"I wanted it, yes," Veta says softly, touching her lips.

"Have you ever been kissed?"

"Yes," she says. "But it felt wrong. Like you weren't thinking about me."

How did she see right through me? "I need some air." I turn and hurry out the door, with Veta following behind.

"What do you want from me, Veta?" I ask, keeping my gaze on the ground.

"I want you to allow me to love you," she says, reaching out, her fingers brushing my arm. But it's not the touch I long to feel. "I want you to love me in return. I want us to be married, to start a family, right here where we belong."

Meeting her hazel eyes, I will myself to feel something for this woman who's poured out her heart to me. But there's nothing. "How do you know that you'd be happy with me?"

"I've loved you for most of my life."

I shake my head slowly. "Veta, you don't know who I am. Or what I've become."

"Please, don't say no." A tear slips down her cheek. "We'll be good together." She cups my face with her hand. "I've dreamt about what it would be like for so many years. I know you'll be kind and gentle."

"Are you still a virgin, Veta?"

She looks down, her voice barely a whisper. "No. But please, don't tell Mama."

The weight of her words sinks in, but I keep my expression unreadable. In this village, tradition and reputation are everything. If anyone finds out she hasn't saved herself for marriage, her prospects will vanish. The men here value purity over character, and that disgusts me more than I care to admit.

"Your secret is safe," I say, my voice steady, though my gaze sharpens. "But understand this—I'm not the kind of man who handles a woman gently."

She hesitates, then lifts her eyes to meet mine. There's determination there, defiance even. "You can teach me," she says softly, stepping closer. Her fingers brush mine as she tries to grab my hand.

I pull away sharply, retreating before she can close the gap.

"We can go inside now," she continues, undeterred. Her voice takes on a pleading edge. "I'll show you that I can please you."

"Veta," I snap, my tone harsher than intended. Her lips part in surprise, but I don't stop. "This isn't a game. You don't know what you're asking for."

Part of me longs to take her up on her offer. To go inside and sink into her, all while envisioning she's Natalie. I want to fuck her until the pain in my heart is gone. But I can't. Veta deserves more than to be used by a man who's in love with someone else.

Her cheeks flush, whether from embarrassment or frustration, I can't tell. "I'm not a child. I know what I want," she insists, her voice trembling slightly.

"You don't," I counter, the steel in my voice leaving no room for argument. I take a deliberate step back, putting more space between us. "I can't do this right now."

"I understand." Her eyes shine with unshed tears. For a brief moment, I see the fragility behind her boldness, the cracks in the facade she's trying so desperately to hold together. "You've been so focused on Anoushka you haven't thought about your own needs," she says softly. "Please, let me take care of you." Her hands move to my pants, but I grab them first.

"This isn't about what you want." My tone softens just enough to temper the sharpness of my earlier words. "I have to go." I can't stay a second longer, or my willpower is liable to falter, and I'll do something I can't take back.

Viktor

Winter is setting in early. It's mid-November, and snow has been falling for the past two days. Veta still comes by each day to help with *Babusya*. She's not said anything more about us, but I see the longing in her eyes. I feel it when she brushes up against me. But I don't return her affection.

Babusya's been clinging to life, but each day, she slips further away. I know our time together is almost up. She hasn't been able to get out of bed, let alone sit up, for over a week. She's stopped eating, barely drinks, and spends her days in restless sleep, murmuring for *Dido*.

I spend my days by her side, holding her hand and talking to her about all the memories she and I share—the warmth of her kitchen and the stories she told me as a child. And I tell her about Natalie and Rose so that when she passes, she'll become their guardian angel, protecting them in ways I no longer can. Above all, I need her to know she's not alone.

"Illya is here," she whispers suddenly. Her shaky hand points toward the door. "He's calling for me."

My chest tightens. I've heard it said that just before a person passes, they see loved ones waiting for them.

"*Babusya*, please don't leave me," I plead, the words tumbling out in a broken whisper. The tears I've tried to hold back stream freely now, unstoppable. "I don't want to be alone."

Her gaze softens, though it seems far away. "Your mama and papa are with him," she murmurs, her tone laced with an other-worldly certainty.

I draw in a shaky breath, forcing myself to be strong. She doesn't deserve to carry my pain into the next world. "I know you have to go," I manage, though the words threaten to shatter me. "I'll be brave. Just like you always told me to be."

My heart shatters, but I press on. "You don't need to worry about me. Please, tell Mama and Papa I love them. Go to *Dido*." My voice cracks, and I swipe at the tears blurring my vision. "I will always love you, *Babusya*." I lean in, pressing a kiss to her weathered cheek, my lips trembling against her skin.

"*Vitya*, my boy," she whispers. "*Ya tebe lyublyu.*"

Her chest rises and falls in a final, ragged breath. Then her hand goes limp in mine.

Her last words to me, *I love you*, are a comfort I cling to even as grief crushes me. She's gone, but her spirit lingers. I feel it, faint but real, in the stillness of the room.

I hold her hand, unwilling to let go, even though she already has. The ache in my chest deepens with every moment that passes. She was my last remaining family. And now she's gone.

This time, I'm truly alone.

As is tradition, *Babusya's* viewing lasts for three days. Villagers visit to pay their respects to the woman many viewed as their own grandmother. Her funeral takes place in the village's small stone church, which is overflowing with people. Some have traveled from neighboring villages. Every face in the crowd reflects the love and admiration they felt for her.

During the service, I take a moment to speak. The grief in their eyes is heavy, but I force myself to meet it.

"*Babusya* was born and raised in this village," I begin. "She raised my mama here, and after my parents died, she raised me here, too. When I found out she was sick, I begged her to go to a bigger city with me, but she refused," I pause, a faint smile breaking through the sorrow. "She was always stubborn."

A quiet chuckle ripples through the room.

"I was prepared to drag her away kicking and screaming, if necessary, until someone I respect very much reminded me that I had to honor her wishes. I owed her at least that much for the unconditional love she'd always given to me. I owed her the right to leave this world where and how she chose." I pause, trying to control my emotions.

I stop for a moment, gathering myself, my hands gripping the podium tightly. "The past few months have been some of the best and worst of my life. I spent every moment I could with her. She told me her stories one last time, and I committed them to memory. And even though I didn't want her to leave, I had the chance to tell her how much I loved her. I was able to say goodbye."

My voice falters. No longer able to contain my emotions, I nod to the priest and step back to my seat in silence.

After the service, *Babusya* is laid to rest beside her husband. I stand by her grave while villagers take turns saying their final goodbyes, each one leaving flowers on the freshly turned soil. When the last mourner departs, I linger, staring at the mound of earth that now separates us.

Back at the house, the emptiness is suffocating. The echoes of her presence—her voice, her laughter—are replaced by the deafening silence of loss. The walls hold only ghosts now, whispers of memories that refuse to fade.

I throw open my bedroom door and drag my bag out from under the bed. Pulling open the drawers, I toss my clothes into it haphazardly. I don't care about order. I need to leave. The ride back to Belgorod will be cold, but I don't care. Anything is better than staying in this hollow shell of a home.

Helmet in hand, I move toward the door, only to find Yelyzaveta standing on the other side. Her eyes flick to the bag in my hand, and her face falls.

"Are you leaving?"

"Yes."

"There are more feasts. The mourning period isn't over."

"For me, it is."

"I was hoping you'd stay." Her voice is soft, but there's a desperate edge to it. "That you'd give us a chance."

"Veta," I say, forcing my tone to remain even, "you're a beautiful woman. I'll always be grateful for the love and care you showed *Babusya*."

"I can take care of you, too," she pleads, following me as I step toward my bike. "Just let me. Please don't leave me again."

"I'm not the man for you, Veta." I swing my leg over my bike and get adjusted on the seat.

"But you are." She grabs onto my arm. "Stop for a minute. Try to remember all the good times we've shared."

I stop, staring at her for a long moment. "That was a long time ago."

"It can be like that again," she insists.

I pull my helmet on. "No, it can't."

"If you won't stay," she says, her voice desperate now, "then let me come with you. We'll be so good together. Just give me a chance."

I start the bike. The roar of the engine drowns out her voice. Her lips move, her tears falling freely, but I can't hear her anymore. And I don't want to. I have no more feelings. The last of them died with *Babusya*.

Pulling down the face shield of my helmet, I rev the bike and drive away. Veta's reflection lingers in my mirror. She's dropped to her knees in the snow, her arms wrapped around herself as she weeps. Good. Let her see me for the bastard I am. Let her hate me.

It's better this way. She deserves someone who will choose her, someone who'll love her the way she deserves.

At the edge of the village, I pull my cell from my pocket and toss it to the ground. The bike's tires crunch over it with ease.

I don't want anyone from my past to contact me. No one to follow me. It's better for everyone if I disappear.

Viktor Dobrow no longer exists.

It's time to become someone else and go back to work.

Viktor

Six months. That's how long I've been living in Belgorod, undergoing a transformation. My hair, now shoulder-length, is a darker shade of blond thanks to a wash in color. Brown contact lenses mask my blue eyes, helping me disappear into the crowd.

I don't need the money. My time with Maxim ensured I never have to work again, but I can't stand sitting around with nothing to do. I'm not going back to work for Max. So, I'm on a job hunt. Men like me don't scroll job sites and email a polished resume. The kind of work I'm seeking is buried in the darkest corners of the internet.

I set up a profile under the name *The Nightingale*. To most, the bird is an innocent songbird known for its haunting melody. But it carries a darker mythology. Legend says when the Nightingale sings at night, it connects to shadows and danger. Enemies fear its song. I've felt connected to the bird for many years, and wear its image on my back.

Since setting up my profile, I've had several offers. But I'm in no rush. Run-of-the-mill hit jobs or vengeful spouses don't interest me. I'm waiting for something that feels right.

I'm in the middle of my daily workout when my phone buzzes. A notification pops up: a new request addressed to *The Nightingale*. My instincts stir—this is it. The one I've been waiting for. I slip my phone back into my shorts pocket, not wanting prying eyes at the gym to catch a glimpse. Quickly wiping down the equipment, I head for my apartment.

Once there, I open the email.

Nightingale,

The target: Saimir Hasani, second in command for a breakoff clan of the Kompania Bello crime syndicate. Reply to this message if you are interested.

John Smith

Sitting back in my chair, I run my hands through my hair as I process the name. The Kompania Bello—Albanian Mafia. Their reputation is brutal. Other criminal organizations steer clear of them for a reason. Too unpredictable. Too violent. There's an old saying in this world: don't fuck with the Albanians.

This is exactly what I've been waiting for.

Mr. Smith,

You've piqued my interest. What's the job?

Nightingale.

I'm halfway through making dinner when the next notification arrives. I wipe my hands on a towel and open the email.

Nightingale,

Duke Henry and Duchess Adelaide of Southerland live on a private island off the coast of Grenada. Recently, their daughter, Lady Clare, went missing while vacationing on the mainland. She vanished from a nightclub, and after weeks of searching, she was found—alive, but barely. She'd been raped, beaten, and drugged repeatedly.

The person responsible? Saimir Hasani.

Lady Clare remembers meeting him at the club. He invited her for a walk on the beach, to which she agreed. The next thing she recalls is waking up in a concrete cell. Hasani marked her body, kept her drugged, and planned to traffic her. The family found her before he could sell her, but the damage was done. She's home now, but she's not recovering well.

Hasani's still in the area, protected by his clan. This will not be a quick or easy job.

The bounty is $20,000,000.

Are you interested?

John Smith

A wave of cold fury surges through me as I read. Another predator who thought he could take whatever he wanted. Am I interested in wiping another trafficking piece of shit off the earth? Yes. I don't delay my reply.

Mr. Smith

I'm the man for the job. Send the details—I'm ready to leave immediately.

As for Lady Clare, tell her family to contact Jelena's Hope in St. Petersburg. Ask for Maxim Solonik. Let them know an old friend referred them. He'll make sure she gets the help she needs.

Nightingale.

Viktor

AFTER NEARLY FOURTEEN HOURS IN THE AIR, THE plane's wheels finally touch down in Grenada. My passport reads James Anderson, a Canadian software engineer who's grown tired of bitter winters and is ready for life in the Caribbean. The cover story is simple. I'll be staying at Hasani's resort while I *look for an apartment*. In reality, I'll be hunting for the perfect opportunity to take him out.

Maurice Bishop Airport is smaller than I expected. Its simplicity reminds me of Northmeadow, the airport I flew into countless times with Natalie.

Stop, Viktor. I shut down the thought before it can take root. This isn't the time or place. James Anderson doesn't know Natalie. I need to focus.

As I walk through the single terminal, I spot a man holding a sign with my alias on it: James Anderson. Approaching him, I nod, and he silently takes my bag. We head to a waiting car, the quiet stretching until we're on the road.

Finally, he speaks. "Saimir Hasani owns the Island Spice Resort. You'll be staying in one of their private villas. The main resort building houses The Cinnamon Room, one of the most popular clubs on the island. It's also where Lady Clare was last seen before her disappearance." He glances at me. "Before you ask, Hasani also controls the local authorities."

"Saimir Hasani is the owner of the Island Spice Resort. You'll be staying in one of their private villas. In the main resort building is The Cinnamon Room, one of the most popular clubs on the island. Hasani is known to keep a strong presence there. It's the same club Lady Clare disappeared from. Before you ask, Hasani also owns the local authorities."

Keeping my tone neutral, I ask, "Where do I fit in?"

"Hasani is currently in the market for a new security system for his club. As an upstanding member of the community," he says the words with an edge of sarcasm, "he's appalled a young woman was kidnapped from his establishment. He's eager to ensure the safety of future guests."

"And you're expecting me to sell it to him?"

"During the day, the club doubles as a computer lounge for resort patrons. You'll have a series of well-timed phone calls regarding the security software you're supposedly developing. The goal is for Hasani to overhear and inquire about your services."

I raise an eyebrow. "You think he'll take the bait?"

"He's desperate," the driver explains. "He screwed up when he took Lady Clare. She wasn't his usual target—too high-profile. Her face and the club were plastered all over the news. His clan may protect him, but he's still scrambling to cover his tracks. You'll appear as an unsuspecting foreigner, completely unaware of his reputation. He'll see you as an easy mark."

I lean back, considering this. "Mr. Smith didn't mention my supposed career. I don't know the first thing about software."

"There's a laptop bag with your luggage in the trunk. It's preloaded with everything you'll need, including a state-of-the-art security system that you're in the market to sell. All you have to do is press a button during your 'demos,' and the computer does the rest. Use your charm to build rapport with Hasani."

"You make it sound easy."

The driver's tone turns dry. "Hasani's desperate, careless, and in over his head. Your villa's been stocked with everything you'll need to complete the job."

Something about his phrasing makes my jaw tighten. "You're not suggesting I open fire in the middle of a resort, are you? If that's the plan, turn the car around. I'm not putting innocent lives at risk."

He glances at me, his expression impassive. "Hasani occupies the entire top floor of the main building. He has a private outdoor space. Your options are a sniper shot from the ground or something close-range if you secure an invitation to his penthouse."

The car rolls to a stop in front of the resort. He shifts into park, then turns to me. "Let me grab your bags and show you to your room, Mr. Anderson."

I nod and step out, glancing up at the resort's facade. On the surface, this job seems straightforward: get in, earn Hasani's trust, and eliminate him. But the glaring omission in all this is the exit strategy. How do I get out alive?

Maybe that's the point.

Only someone with a death wish would take a job like this.

And that describes me.

Death would be an improvement to the hell I'm currently living.

Viktor

I COULD EASILY GET USED TO THIS CAREFREE LIFESTYLE. I wake up just as the sun is peeking over the horizon. Most days, I swim laps in my private pool or run on the beach. I'm just a guy on vacation laying low and getting a feel for the place.

So far, everything's just as I've been told. By day, the Cinnamon Room is filled with businesspeople whose faces are glued to their laptops or cell phone screens. Men who should be enjoying paradise instead of being slaves to their jobs.

Today, I'll be among this group of overachievers. I'm sporting khaki pants and a white linen shirt. My hair is up in the proverbial "man bun." My reflection is unrecognizable to me. I guess that's a good thing. If I can't recognize myself, no one else will be able to either. Grabbing my laptop bag, I walk along the flower-lined path to the resort's main building.

The aesthetic of this place isn't lost on me. It's a clean, modern resort situated on the beautiful turquoise waters of Grand Anse Beach. There're several private units, like mine, with infinity edge pools that appear as though they're spilling into the sea. In addition, the main building is twenty floors high.

The villas are high-end for the resort's wealthier guests, while the rooms in the main building are the more traditional hotel-like rooms. On the main floor are several restaurants, and the place I'm headed—The Cinnamon Room.

When I open the club's door, I'm hit with a gust of cold air. It's stale compared to the trade winds that flow through my villa. No one bothers to look up. Each is engrossed in their digital world. I find a table in the corner where I can sit with my back to the wall, giving me a clear view of the room. Pulling out my laptop, I get to work—whatever that's supposed to mean.

I find an encrypted email program and a note from Mr. Smith welcoming me to the island and advising me that the first install-ment of my salary has been deposited into my account. I log into my bank to ensure the money's there.

Usually, I'd have Dimitri do some digging to find who's behind the mask. But since we're not in contact, I'm trusting in an unknown. This time, the money's where it's supposed to be.

I occupy myself searching for information on Saimir Hasani. He's the second in command of his clan and has a reputation for his cocky attitude and sloppy work. Despite that, the Albanians are tight-knit, and they protect their own. No matter how unpop-ular Hasani may be, his clan will defend his life to the death.

My first goal is to meet Hasani and get into his good graces. If the intel I have is correct, not a day goes by that he doesn't make an appearance.

A young, attractive waitress approaches my table. "Can I get you anything to eat or drink?"

"I'll take a coffee."

"Sure. I'll be right back." She smiles and sashays her hips as she walks away.

I return my attention to my computer and do some more reading about Hasani. Several minutes later, the waitress returns, placing a steaming mug on the table.

"Do you need anything else?"

"No. Thank you."

I spend most of the afternoon in the Cinnamon room, but there's no sign of Hasani. As each hour passes, the room grows emptier. If I stay too much longer, it may draw unwanted attention. I decide to follow suit and pack it up for the day. Tomorrow, I'll be back to do this all over again.

Viktor

I'M GETTING READY FOR ANOTHER DAY IN MY makeshift office when I receive an email from Mr. Smith letting me know a real estate agent will be here shortly to show me some properties—we must keep up the ruse. Moments later, there's a knock on my villa door. Opening it, I find an attractive woman on the other side.

"Mr. Anderson?"

"Yes."

"I'm Bianca, the realtor. Are you ready to go look at some properties?"

"Please, call me James. And yes, I can't wait to see what's available."

As Bianca and I make our way through the main lobby, a man steps out of an office and walks toward us.

"Mr. Anderson. Allow me to introduce myself. I'm Saimir Hasani."

I find it interesting that he knows who I am and has chosen to make his presence known today.

"It's a pleasure to meet you." We shake hands.

"Are you planning on leaving us?"

"What do you mean?"

"You are with Ms. Bianca, one of the island's top real estate brokers. So, I assumed you were going to look at properties. Unless I've interrupted something else?" He doesn't hide his perusal of her body. She stiffens beside me. Clearly, his reputation precedes him.

"Although this resort is gorgeous, I'm in the market for permanent housing."

"That's a shame. I was hoping we'd be able to spend some time together. I've been informed you have a product I'm in the market for."

"I see," I say flatly.

"Perhaps you can alter your plans so we can discuss the opportunity?"

"That won't be possible. I promised my afternoon to Bianca. Maybe we can meet tomorrow instead?"

Hasani looks surprised that I've turned down his offer. I don't want to appear too eager—desperate. And I want to get Bianca out of here as quickly as possible.

"Ms. Bianca is more than welcome to join us."

"Mr. Anderson, if you'd rather—"

"Mr. Hasani, I'm sure you understand Bianca has cleared her schedule today to show me available properties on the island. It would be rude of me to waste her time talking software." I give her a smile and a slight nod of my head. "I am free tomorrow afternoon if that fits into your schedule?"

Although he appears to be keeping his cool. I don't fail to notice the vein pulsing in his neck. This man is not used to being told no. "I will meet you in the Cinnamon Room tomorrow afternoon."

"That should work for me. I'll see you tomorrow." I place my hand on Bianca's back. "Shall we?"

Although I don't turn around, I feel Hasani's eyes boring into our backs as we walk away from him.

Once we get outside, Bianca turns to me. "Do you realize who that was?"

"I've heard his name mentioned. He owns part of the resort or something."

"Saimir Hasani is not a man you want to cross or say no to."

"I'll make a note of that. Are you ready to look at apartments?"

Maxim

"There you are," I say as I walk into the indoor swimming pool room and find Svetlana just climbing out of the pool. "I've been looking all over for you."

"What's up?"

"Have you heard from Viktor recently?"

"No. We aren't exactly on speaking terms."

"Have you spoken to Natalie or Alex?"

"I talked to Natalie yesterday." Svetlana wraps herself in a towel and sits on one of the poolside chairs. "Why?"

"Did she say anything about him?"

"Why the inquisition about Viktor?"

"He's been out of touch for quite a while."

Svetlana rolls her eyes. "Viktor's a big boy. He can take care of himself."

I am a patient man, but my daughter and her flippant attitude toward everyone and everything is beginning to wear on my last nerve. I was hoping that by giving her some time and space, she would open up and tell us what was troubling her, but she has not. Rather than opening up, she is becoming more closed off.

I sit in the chair next to her. "When are you going to tell us the real reason you came home?"

"Because Brandon and I broke up." She sounds like a broken record. "I had my fun in the States and decided it was time to come home."

I study her closely, looking for any hint that could give me a clue as to what is troubling my daughter, but she gives me none.

Svetlana stands and puts her hands on her hips. "Why is it so hard to believe I wanted to come home?"

"We thought things were going well with you and Brandon. Then, one day, you show up at home with no explanation to him or to us."

"Everyone's always taking his side. No one cares about what I want or how I feel. Forget it. I can't do this again." She tosses her towel and storms out of the room.

I am left confused. I would love to know what my daughter is feeling. However, she refuses to let anyone in.

And I still have no answers as to Viktor's whereabouts.

Viktor

Bianca and I spend the afternoon looking at incredible properties. If I was really in the market, I'd have difficulty choosing.

"Do you want to see any more today?"

"You've given me a lot to think about. Let's call it a day."

"Would you like to stop and get a bite to eat? I can show you one of my favorite restaurants."

I've had quite an enjoyable day with Bianca. She's not only beautiful, we've not found ourselves at a loss for anything to talk about. In another life, I'd be crazy to turn this woman down. But I'm not looking for friendship or love—that would further complicate an already difficult situation.

I'm here for one reason—to kill Saimir Hasani. Anyone conceived as being connected to me could find themselves in the line of fire.

"That's a very kind offer, but I'll have to pass."

"Oh," she says quietly and looks down. "I just thought—"

"Bianca, I've had a great time with you this afternoon, but I'm engaged." I lie. "My fiancé stayed behind until I find a permanent place here."

"I'm so sorry. I had no idea."

"It's fine. No harm done."

Our driver pulls up in front of the resort. "I'll give you a call as soon as I make a decision."

"Thank you, James."

I get out and watch as the car pulls away. I saw the way Hasani looked at her earlier. I don't want her anywhere near this place.

When I walk inside, Hasani's standing in the main lobby talking with several men. I can tell the second I'm spotted as the group stops talking, and Hasani makes his way over to me.

"Welcome back, Mr. Anderson. How was your tour?"

"It's a beautiful island. Several places look promising. If you'll excuse me, I have some business I need to attend to."

"What time should I expect you tomorrow?"

"I have several phone conferences scheduled for the first half of the day." I purposely don't give him a definite answer. "I'll be down as soon as my schedule permits."

"I'm a very busy man, Mr. Anderson."

"As am I, Mr. Hasani. Now, if you'll excuse me, I need to get back to my room."

He steps aside, allowing me to pass. As I walk away, he and the men he's with begin speaking in what I can only assume is Albanian.

This is the first I've seen other Albanians hanging around here. Although I was able to get a good look at them, this could pose a significant problem for me. The more I'm outnumbered, the more difficult it will be to plan an exit strategy that gives me even a slight chance of survival.

With their faces fresh in my mind, I head back to my villa, hoping to identify the new characters in the game.

I WAS ABLE TO POSITIVELY IDENTIFY TWO OUT OF THREE of the men Hasani was talking with earlier. The first is Ismael Hasani, Saimir's younger brother, and the third in command. From what I read, those two are very tight. Although Saimir holds a higher rank, Ismael is the brains of the operation and often makes the more important decisions. Saimir is merely his puppet.

The second man is Elion Tehiri, the clan leader. Since Lady Clare's kidnapping, Elion has kept a more public presence.

The third man is a mystery. I can't find his picture or any information on him. I don't like having unknowns.

If it were almost any other mafia outlet, I'd look for the power-hungry man. The one who's willing to take out the person blocking their climb to the top. The problem for me is the lengths Albanians will go to protect one of their own. Ismael is both clan and blood. I'll never find an in there, and Elion would just as soon take me out before turning on Hasani.

I'm on my own. As long as I take him out first, exact justice on Hasani for what he did to an innocent young woman, I'll gladly take a bullet.

After rehearsing the script I was given to sell the security program, I check the time. It's half past two. I figure I've made

Hasani wait long enough. Sliding my laptop into its bag, I slowly walk to the Cinnamon Room. Hasani has thirty minutes to show. First rule of the game is that we play by my rules.

I pull the door open and take a quick look around. It's relatively empty today compared to most other days. I head to the table in the corner and settle in. The same waitress that's here every day smiles when she sees me and starts walking over, but I wave her off.

I pull out my laptop and get to work. My senses are on high alert. I'm uncertain how Hasani knew my name and about the security program. I have a feeling there's more going on than meets the eye. This is where working on my own is risky. I don't have Dimitri and his tech skills to fall back on. No one has my back. If I make it out of this alive, I'll have to form a new team, people I'll be able to trust.

"Mr. Anderson, I'm glad you found time for me today." Hasani catches me off guard. I need to be more careful.

"How can I help you?" I sit back in my chair and cross my arms.

"I've heard you are selling a highly sophisticated security program. Is that true?"

"Possibly."

"I'm in the market for that exact product." He waves over the young waitress. "Bring Mr. Anderson and I both a *Skrapar*."

"Yes, sir." She bows her head.

"I'll just have some water," I say before she walks away.

The girl looks to Hasani, who nods before she scurries away.

"Are you not a fan?" he asks.

"I don't mix alcohol and business." My gaze goes to the young girl pouring our drinks at the bar.

He glances over his shoulder. "She's an attractive little thing, isn't she?" Hasani turns back to me.

"She's a bit young."

"Young and moldable is my preference," he says deadpan. "Now, let's discuss your product."

I've rehearsed the script so many times I see it in my sleep. Right now, I'm thankful for that because my words come out confident and unhurried. I stop talking while the girl sets our drinks on the table and resume my sales pitch once she walks away.

"Your product sounds too good to be true." Hasani is nearly salivating.

"I assure you that is not the case." Before continuing, I look around the room. "I'm sure you already have a security system, and your business looks to cater to high-class clientele. May I ask why you would require such sophisticated software?"

"Several months ago, a young woman was kidnapped from my club." He looks me dead in the eyes as he spins his tale. "As you can imagine, that is not the reputation I wish for my resort to have. My responsibility to the community and my guests is to ensure nothing like that happens again. I intend to have the best security system money can buy."

"I see." I don't break his stare. If it's a battle of wills, I'll be coming out on top. And I do. Hasani is the first to look away. "Would you like to see a demonstration?"

"Yes." He sits up straighter, obviously excited at the prospect of moving forward.

While I show him the slides and explain the capabilities of my product, I also keep an eye on the people around us. During our meeting, the same three men Hasani was talking to earlier have each meandered in. They're seated at separate tables, laptops in front of them, facing our direction. It's clear I'm being watched.

"So, as you see, this product will take care of both digital security and video surveillance inside and outside your resort. The data will be transferred to an encrypted server that's impenetrable from cyberattacks."

"How much will all this cost me?"

"Five million," I say flatly.

"That's a steep price." He raises an eyebrow.

I'm not willing to negotiate. "I understand if your guests'

safety and your reputation are not worth that much." I close my laptop and start to slide it back into the bag. "It was—"

"Where are you off to in such a hurry? I didn't turn your offer down."

I set the bag aside, leaving the laptop on the table.

"Typically, I don't do business with people I don't know. In my line of work, you can never be too careful. And five million is a large sum of money." He taps his fingers on the table. "I'm having a little get-together with some friends and other business associates in my penthouse this evening. Why don't you join us? It'll give us a chance to get better acquainted."

"What time?"

"Seven."

This time, I put the laptop in the bag and stand. "I'll be there."

Maxim

I HAVE ASKED EVERYONE I THOUGHT MIGHT HAVE heard from Viktor and received the same answer. Nothing. Viktor has not been in contact with anyone. My texts have been left unread. His voicemail box is now full. He asked for space, and I have given him that for over six months. But in our line of work, when a person is unreachable, it usually signals they are in trouble.

I did not want to resort to this, but I am left with no other choice. I must enlist the help of Dimitri.

"Hey, boss. What's up?" he asks when I enter the tech room.

"Have you heard from Viktor?"

"No. We're not exactly friends these days." He turns his attention back to his screen.

That is the same story I am hearing from everyone. It seems as though Viktor has not only physically disappeared but has also cut everyone who cares about him out of his life.

"Why do you ask?"

"He has dropped off the radar. I am unable to contact him. Can you locate him with your tracking software?"

Dimitri developed a tracking program that has been installed on the phones of all my employees.

"Sure."

He pulls up another screen. It is a database of all my employees. He clicks on Viktor's name and attempts to locate his phone. This kind of technology is not my forte, but I can tell something is wrong. Dimitri flips through several screens before spinning his chair around.

"There's no signal from his phone. It hasn't sent info in months."

I was afraid of something like this. "We need to find him."

"Is he in trouble?"

"I am not certain."

"I'll get right on it." Dimitri starts the process of locating Viktor.

If anyone can locate Viktor, it is my nephew.

Viktor

I'M STRESSED ABOUT TONIGHT AND NEED TO WORK OFF my nerves. When I return to my villa, I change and go for a run on the beach. I don't know why this job is shaking me. It's an uncomfortable feeling. Things can go wrong quickly if I don't stay in the right head space. I don't have a team to fall back on. This is all on me.

After my run, I shower and put on some dress clothes. When I check the time on my cell, it's a little after seven. Show time.

When I arrive at the penthouse, I'm greeted by security, who pats me down for weapons and then checks my name off the guest list.

Hasani's penthouse is enormous and ornately decorated. People mill about, drinks in hand, while calypso music plays in the background. The entire front wall of the penthouse is made of several large sets of doors that allow easy passage from inside to the large outdoor terrace.

A server walks by carrying a tray with glasses of both red and white wine. I grab a glass of red wine. I won't be drinking much, but I at least need to look the part. I wander around the inside room, making mental notes of the placement of the security cameras before making my way outside.

I finally spot Hasani speaking with a small group of men. One of them is his brother Ismael. Two women are hanging on his arms, giggling at everything he says. I force myself not to roll my eyes at their desperation.

When Hasani looks up and spots me, he shakes the girls off his arm and makes his way in my direction. The girls don't seem upset. They move on to the next man.

"Mr. Anderson, welcome to my home."

"Nice place."

"Follow me. I want to introduce you to my brother." I follow him over to the group he was speaking with. "Ismael. This is Mr. Anderson, the software developer I was telling you about."

"Please call me James," I say to both men. "It's a pleasure to meet you, Ismael." I put my hand out.

Hesitantly, he returns the gesture. "My brother tells me you're from the Czech Republic. How did you end up here?"

"Your brother must've misheard. I'm from Canada."

"Your accent says otherwise." Ismael eyes me suspiciously.

"My family is originally from the Soviet Union. Before I was born, they fled from the communist regime and settled in Canada."

"I see. And how is it you ended up here?"

"I got sick of Canadian winters." I chuckle. "Since I work for myself, I can live anywhere." Realizing it's a test, I don't break eye contact. "How I ended up here is an interesting story. I was out with a few of my friends. Admittedly, we'd had a little too much to drink. They dared me to spin the globe and move wherever my finger landed—Grenada it was. I'm thankful I landed in a warm area. I could've ended up in Saskatchewan."

"You're a man not afraid of taking risks?" Hasani asks.

"I have nothing to lose." I shrug.

"You have no family?" Ismael inquires.

"My parents died in a car accident several years ago, and I've never married." I make a show of perusing the bodies of the women who have reattached themselves to Hasani. "I prefer to sample merchandise. I've not found anyone worth keeping after a night or two."

"We only offer the finest delicacies." Ismael's serious demeanor cracks. "I'm sure my brother can offer you a sample to try."

"Give me your requirements, and I'll ensure it's delivered to your door." Hasani smiles.

"Let's table this discussion for another time. I don't want to monopolize your attention this evening."

"If you gentlemen will excuse me," Hasani says. "I see another business associate I need to speak to. So I'll leave you two to get better acquainted."

Ismael watches as his brother walks away. "Saimir tells me you've designed an impenetrable security system." He wastes no time getting back to business.

I'm thankful the conversation has changed. The *merchandise* Hasani deals in is hanging on the arms of multiple men in the room tonight. It chills me to my core, knowing these women are not here of their own free will, and there's nothing I can do to stop it on my own.

"Yes, I have." I deliver my practiced speech with ease. Ismael, like his brother, hangs on my every word. "As you see, my program will give you the ability to have hidden eyes and ears on every inch of this property while ensuring the security feed is impenetrable."

"When can we see your product in action?"

"I can arrange for a small-scale demonstration this week. I'll need the club closed to guests while my team installs the equipment."

"I'll make sure the club is closed on Monday. Will that work?"

"I'll get in touch with my team and make the arrangements."

Viktor

Parties are not my scene on a good day. Knowing I was being tested and watched all night only increased the stress. When I returned to my villa, I was exhausted. Before I passed out, I sent a message to Mr. Smith to have his team here early Monday morning for a trial installation. I don't wait for his reply before I power off the phone and fall asleep.

Morning comes far too quickly. I wish I was the kind of person who could sleep half of the day, but that's never been me. I reach over to the nightstand and grab my phone to power it on. The reply to last night's text is waiting for me.

Mr. Smith: I'm impressed by how quickly you work. My team will be there Monday morning with the necessary equipment.

Nightingale: How many men should I expect?
Mr. Smith: Two.

So far, things are moving along smoothly—too smoothly. Which concerns me. When things go this easy, there's usually a problem. But from everything I see, there's none. The bio and history of James Anderson are solid.

A knock on my villa door interrupts my thoughts. I throw my legs over the bed and pad over to the door in my boxers. It's most likely housekeeping. I'll ask them to come back later. I'm caught off guard when I see it's the young waitress from the club, and she's holding a tray.

"I have your breakfast, sir. Compliments of Mr. Hasani."

"How thoughtful of him." I reach for the tray.

"I'm sorry, sir. I was told to bring it into your room." She picks up an envelope from the tray and hands it to me. "This is for you."

"Come in." I step aside, allowing her to pass. Inside the envelope, there's a handwritten note.

Mr. Anderson,

My brother spoke very highly of you. I look forward to working together in the near future. Please accept this complimentary breakfast. It comes with a sampling of the best delicacies we have to offer.

S. Hasani

It doesn't take much effort to read between the lines. The delicacy included with my breakfast is the woman who delivered it. When I turn around, I find her unbuttoning her shirt.

"Stop," I say. "What's your name?"

She looks up at me with expressive brown eyes. "Crystal."

"What's your real name?"

"I don't know what you mean."

"Are you here of your own free will?"

"Yes," she answers hesitantly.

"Please sit down." I pull a chair out from the table for her and then take a seat across from her. "Have you eaten today?"

"Yes, sir." She looks down at her folded hands.

"Whatever your boss told you will happen here today will not happen."

Her body goes rigid. She's clearly afraid.

"Look at me, please.".

Slowly, she lifts her head, and her gaze meets mine.

"I'm not going to risk your safety. I'll tell your boss how pleased I am. Will that help?"

She nods.

"Now, tell me your real name?"

She looks around the room nervously.

"There are no cameras in here." That's the first thing I checked for when I arrived.

"Jessica," she says quietly.

"How old are you, Jessica?"

"Twenty-three."

I run my hands through my hair. "Are you from Grenada, Jessica?"

She shakes her head.

"Where are you from?"

Jessica drops her gaze once again.

"I know that you have no reason to trust me. But I promise you I won't tell Hasani anything."

"I used to live in New York City."

Her words are like a dagger in my heart. Of all the places she could've been from, it had to be there. "How did you end up here?"

"It was four years ago, and I was in my second year of college and was offered the opportunity to study abroad—Paris. It was like a dream come true." The corner of her mouth lifts in a small smile. "I met a wealthy man. He was gorgeous and was so nice to me. We had a whirlwind romance." She shakes her head. "I was so naïve. I put my complete trust in a stranger. One evening, we went sailing on his yacht. I don't remember anything until I woke up here."

"Is that man still here?"

"He comes and goes. Mr. Hasani sends him to get the girls."

"Is he here right now?"

"No. He's been gone for a week or so."

"Dammit." I slam my hands on the table, startling Jessica. "I'm sorry. I didn't mean to frighten you." I take the lids off the plates. There's an array of both hot and cold breakfast dishes. Jessica can't take her eyes off the food. I give her a plate. "Eat."

"I can't."

"You were sent to please me, right?"

"Yes, sir."

"It would please me to see you eat."

Hesitantly, she puts a few pieces of fresh fruit on her plate. That's when it dawns on me that I'm only wearing boxers. "I'm going to get dressed. Take as much food as you want."

I go to the bedroom, where I shut and lock the door. I'm not taking any chances of this girl following me here so she can follow Hasani's orders.

Once I'm dressed, I sit on the edge of the bed and put my head in my hands. What the hell am I supposed to do? This girl's been trafficked. She'll be safe if she's with me, but I don't know if I can trust her. There's a lot of sensitive information going back and forth in this room. What's worse is knowing there are people who can help her, but I can't call them. Keeping her here is a risk, but sending her back is unthinkable.

"Fuck." The best I can do is keep her with me for the day while I try to devise a better plan.

When I return to the main room, Jessica has a plate full of fruit and a bagel. I sit back down and grab a piece of mango.

"We're going into town today."

"Mr. Hasani won't allow me to leave—"

"Let me take care of Hasani."

I call the number I have programmed into my phone for the Cinnamon room. It's no surprise that Hasani picks up on the first ring.

"Mr. Anderson, I hope you found breakfast to your liking?"

"Your brother was correct when he said you only serve the finest delicacies. I'm honored to have been gifted a sample."

"I'm surprised to hear from you." He chuckles. "I assumed you'd be occupied today."

"I plan to be. I'm taking Crystal into town with me."

"That's a rather unusual request. I normally don't allow guests—"

"It's not a request, Mr. Hasani. Your note said she was sent to please me. Going into town with a beautiful woman on my arm will do just that." I keep my tone flat. "We'll be late. If she bores me, I'll have her back to you tonight. If she manages to keep my attention, we'll discuss other arrangements."

"Do be cautious with her off my property. Whoever took the Dutchess is still at large. I wouldn't want any harm to come to Crystal."

"There's no need for worry. I won't take my eyes off her."

Jessica's body trembles as we walk out the resort's front doors. I hold her tight against me, making it look like we're much better acquainted with one another's bodies.

"Try to relax," I say quietly. "This is just until we're out of Hasani's sight."

"He has eyes everywhere," she whispers.

"There's our ride." I point to the car waiting for us.

We both slide onto the back seat. When I look out the car's window, Ismael stands just outside the resort's doors. I'm going to have to play today very carefully. There's no way Hasani's letting me walk this girl out of here without having us followed.

Maxim

"Boss," Dimitri pops his head in my office. "Do you have a few minutes?"

"Come in." It's been several weeks since I asked him to locate Viktor. I am hoping his presence here means he has some news. Dimitri sits in one of the wingback chairs across from my desk.

"That man knows how to cover his tracks." He sighs.

I do not like the sound of this already. "Do you have any information?"

"He's not good enough to hide from me." Dimitri laughs. "After he left us in St. Petersburg, it seems he went back to Belgorod."

"He has kept an apartment there for many years."

Dimitri looks surprised. Viktor does not like to talk about his past. Even though the men have been friends for many years, it seems there is much Viktor has not told his friend.

"I knew he used to have an apartment. I assumed he got rid of it a long time ago," Dimitri says. "Anyway, the most logical place for me to look after that was Bobrivka. And sure enough, that's the last place his phone had a signal."

"Yes, I knew he was there. He needed to spend time with his grandmother."

"I got in touch with his old friend Yelyzaveta. She's one of the only people in the village with a cell phone. Can you imagine living in today's society without—"

"Dimitri, please try to stay on track."

"While he was there, his grandmother passed away. Veta said he left shortly after."

"And I am to assume he did not tell her where he was going."

"Considering the tears on the phone call, his leaving was not how she saw their future. She said he took off on his bike without so much as looking back."

That sounds very much like Viktor. To this day, he remains haunted by his past. "So, we have hit another dead end."

"Well, not exactly. I was able to get into the security footage from the apartment building." Dimitri smiles proudly. "He spent weeks there." He hands me his cell phone. "Check these out."

I flip through the photographs. Viktor has changed his appearance. He no longer has a bald head but rather shoulder-length dark blond hair and brown eyes. "It does not even resemble the man I know," I say and hand the phone back. "Why would he alter his appearance so drastically?"

"That was my question as well. And, boss, I don't like what I found. Someone in his building had been prowling the dark web, searching for jobs. I accessed some emails from a Mr. Smith to *The Nightingale.*"

I do not like the direction Dimitri's story is heading.

"If *The Nightingale* is who I assume it is, he's taken a job in Grenada going after Saimir Hasani from the Kompania Bello crime syndicate."

"Viktor is going after the Albanian mafia alone? What the fuck is going through his head?" I pound my fist on my desk.

Dimitri fills me in on the details of his assignment—it is a death wish. Viktor is one of the best at his job, but he obviously does not think clearly. Going after the Albanians with a group of men is dangerous, but going after them alone is suicide.

"Where is he?"

"Grenada. He's traveling under an assumed identity, Mr. James Anderson, but facial recognition software isn't fooled by a name." Dimitri pulls up another screen on his phone. "He's undercover as a software engineer and is in the middle of a lucrative deal with Saimir Hasani."

Dimitri further explains how Lady Clare's abduction is related. The puzzle pieces are now coming together. When her parents called, they told us they were sent by an *old friend*. There is only a small group of people who would advise them to use that term. Viktor is one of them. He's there to avenge the harm brought to Lady Clare by killing Hasani.

"He's in way over his head, boss."

"I know." I pause for a moment, thinking over my next move. "You are going after him."

"Me?"

"We cannot send more than one man without attracting unwanted attention," I say thoughtfully. "You have the skills to find him and bring him back. I will call my pilot. You can take the jet to Venezuela. I will arrange for a chartered flight to the island."

Saimir

"Have they left?" I ask Ismael when he walks into my office.

"Yes."

"I don't trust him." I lean back in my chair and tap my finger on my lip. "We're going to search his room while he's gone."

"Do you have someone following them?"

I push the chair back and stand. "You must think I'm *budallaqe.* Of course, I'm having them followed. Let's go."

We meet a member of my cleaning staff on the way. "Have you cleaned Mr. Anderson's room today?"

"No, sir," she answers quickly.

"Why not? He's a very important guest. I don't want him thinking we give any less than the best service."

"Umm," she hesitates. "Mr. Anderson has instructed us not to enter his villa unless he's present."

"I see." That's an interesting bit of information. "Carry on."

She hurries away. Ismael and I look at each other. "It sounds like our Mr. Anderson may be hiding something."

When we get to the villa's door, I instruct Ismael to stand guard. I don't want any surprises while I'm here. Then, I go about searching his room.

At first glance, nothing seems out of the ordinary. His bed is made, and the room is neat and clean. His clothes are hanging in the closet. I search each of the drawers in the bureau but find nothing other than perfectly folded clothes. On the desk is his laptop. Of course, it's password protected. I don't want to waste time there unless I have to.

"I have to be missing something." Looking around, I realize I don't see his luggage. When he checked in, he had a laptop bag and a rolling suitcase. I look in the other storage cabinet but only find his rolling suitcase. Opening it, I find nothing other than a pair of shoes. But I still don't see the bag.

The only place I haven't looked is under the bed. I get down on my knees and move the edge of the bedspread. "There you are," I say, pulling out the black leather bag. Unzipping it, I find a pair of earbuds and an extra charging cord in the main compartment. There are several smaller pockets on the outside. Most of them are empty. Inside the last pocket, I find his passport. It was issued to Mr. James Anderson with his picture. There are several stamps from countries he's visited over the years. Nothing seems amiss.

When I put it back, something dark and shiny catches my eye —a hidden zipper. I open it and pull out another passport. This one has a picture of a man who looks very much like Mr. Anderson, except he's bald with blue eyes. "Viktor Dobrow?" I read the name and then snap a few pictures before carefully putting it back.

Before I leave the room, I take a final look to ensure everything is exactly as I found it. I prefer to maintain the element of surprise.

"Did you find anything?" Ismael asks when I exit the room.

"It seems our Mr. Anderson also goes by Viktor Dobrow."

"When we get back to the office, I'll run the name and his picture through our system and see what we find."

Viktor

"Is there anywhere you want to go?" I ask the young woman sitting next to me.

"I don't know." Jessica looks out the window and then back at me. "I've never been allowed out of the resort," she whispers.

I pull out my phone and do a quick search for tourist activities. Quickly, I spot something that looks fun. I lean forward and show the driver where I want to go. "Can we stop at a shop first? Somewhere, we can get swimsuits."

"No problem," the driver says.

A few minutes later, we're pulling up in front of a store.

"Can you wait for us? We won't be long."

Opening the door, I step out first and look around. Sure enough, a car pulls into a spot not far away. I recognize the face of the driver. He's an employee at the resort. I lean down and take Jessica's hand. "We have some company, so we need to play the part, okay?"

She nods.

When she gets out, she threads her arm through mine.

"Where're we going?" Jessica asks.

"That's a surprise." I smile. "Go pick out a swimsuit and anything else you want."

Jessica gives me a quizzical look. "Are you sure?"

"Unless you want me to pick one out for you. There's a nice one there." I point to some sort of swimsuit with a dress attached to it.

Jessica laughs. "I think I can handle it." She walks over to the rack of women's swimsuits and starts looking through them. While she shops, I grab swim trunks, two beach towels, sunscreen, and a backpack.

Ten minutes later, we've checked out and are ready for our adventure.

It's a short drive to our destination. I've arranged for a private tour of the Seven Sisters Waterfalls.

"James?" A man in a tour guide uniform asks.

"Yes. And this is my girlfriend, Crystal." I don't want to risk saying her real name in case Hasani's man comes asking questions.

"I'm Joaquin. I'll be your guide today." We shake hands. "There are changing rooms over there if you want to put your swimsuits on before we set off on our hike."

We take the opportunity to change and then get on our way.

"This place is beautiful," Jessica says as we walk along jungle-like trails.

"Look over there." I point to a nearby tree. "There's a monkey."

"That's a Mona Monkey. They're native to our island," Joaquin explains. "You're lucky. We don't always see them on our hikes."

We walk in silence for a while until the trail opens to a breathtaking waterfall.

"I'm going to leave you two here to enjoy the water. I'll be back in about an hour."

"Thanks," I say and wait for him to walk away. "Want to go for a swim?"

"Umm..." she hesitates.

"I have no ulterior motives, Jessica. Just a swim."

"Okay."

After taking my shirt and shoes off, I go to the edge of the rock and jump into the turquoise-blue water below. After I resurface, I run my hands through my hair.

"Come on, the water is beautiful."

Jessica takes her shorts and shirt off and stands at the edge of the rock. "I'm scared."

I can't help but stare at her perfect figure in a two-piece swimsuit. Silently chastising myself, I course correct.

"I'm right here. I won't let you get hurt," I encourage. "You can trust me."

"I don't know."

"You can do this."

Jessica shrugs, still uncertain, but then takes the leap. She lands next to me with a splash. I grab her arms, helping her to resurface. When she does, she giggles like a little girl.

"I've never done anything like that. It was incredible."

We swim around for a while, enjoying the crystal-clear water at the bottom of the spectacular waterfall.

"Do you have any family?" she asks.

"My parents died when I was a boy, and I never married."

"I'm sorry," she says quietly.

"What about you? Do you have a family out there?"

"My mom died when I was five. My dad was alive, last I knew, but he won't be looking for me."

"Why not?"

"After mom died, he started drinking. Then, he started using drugs. He didn't pay any attention to me—I was invisible." She pulls herself up on a rock, getting out of the water.

I follow her onto the rock and sit next to her.

"I can't believe a guy that looks like you doesn't have a girl-friend." Her face turns bright red. "Unless you're—"

"I'm not gay if that's what you were going to say." I laugh. "I did have a girl and a baby."

"What happened to them?"

"It was complicated." I don't know what's come over me, but I find myself telling Jessica what happened with Natalie. She's a good listener. There's no judgment on her face. Surprisingly, it feels good to get it out and tell someone who doesn't know either of us.

"Wow," she says when I finish. "That really is complicated. Is that why you came here?"

"Yeah. I needed to get away and clear my head."

A twig snaps, and I jump up, shielding Jessica.

"Did you two enjoy the falls?" Joaquin asks as he makes his way over to us.

I drop my guard and grab a towel, passing the other to Jessica.

"It was amazing. I've never seen anything like it."

"It's time we start making our way back."

Jessica and I grab our things and follow our guide back along the trail. The rest of the hike takes us by the other waterfalls in the area. When we arrive back at the parking lot, I'm relieved to see our driver is still there. I paid the driver well above what he would've made picking up other riders today so that he'd be here when we were done. We slide into the backseat.

"What's the best food around these parts?"

"I know a place." He smiles proudly and starts driving.

After a drive along winding roads, we pull up at a food truck.

"Best food on the island."

Jessica and I enjoy fajitas and crab back.

"Thank you for today, James." She looks at me with tears in her eyes. "I'll never forget it."

The sadness in her brown eyes is almost my undoing. There's no way I'm letting her return to Hasani.

Viktor

WE ARRIVE BACK AT THE RESORT AND ARE BARELY through the front doors when Hasani appears. Jessica tenses beside me.

"Did you two enjoy your day out?" he asks, displeasure evident in his features.

"Ismael's description of your merchandise didn't do it justice." I look over at Jessica, who's staring down at her feet. "How much to keep her for the rest of my stay?"

Jessica gasps.

"You've been very generous with your time and product, Mr. Anderson. I'll throw her in compliments of the resort. However, she'll still need to report to work."

"While she's with me, I want your guarantee no other man will touch her. I don't like to share."

"That can be arranged." Hasani grabs Jessica's hair, forcing her head up. "Can you be a good girl for my friend?"

"Yes, sir," she says quietly.

I grab her arm. "Let's go. I haven't had my fill of you today."

With a hurried pace, I lead her away from Hasani, who's behind us laughing.

When we get back inside the relative safety of my villa, I lock the door and pull the curtains closed. Jessica and I need to have a chat. I'm taking a considerable risk by telling her why I'm really here. I'm hoping if I do, she'll be willing to help me with information on Hasani.

She stands in the middle of the room, nervously playing with her fingers and avoiding eye contact with me.

"Sit down. We need to talk."

Jessica sits on the chair by the desk, and I perch on the edge of the bed. Her face shows no emotion while I explain who I am and what I'm doing here. Yet, even as I speak, I'm second-guessing my decision to trust her with this info. If I'm wrong, this move will cost me my life.

"In exchange for your help and keeping my secret, I'll make sure you're free from Hasani. Do we have a deal?"

Then, I wait.

Silence fills the room as Jessica continues to stare at me. My heart rate increases with each second that goes by.

"Yes, we have a deal," she finally says. "What do I need to do?"

"You need to do what you always do when you work, in addition to keeping an ear out for any conversations that might be of importance." I lean forward, resting my elbows on my spread legs. "I'll take care of the rest."

It's bright and early Monday morning when I get the text that the installation team is here.

"I have to go to the Cinnamon Room for a bit. Keep the door locked. Do not open it for anyone." I hand Jessica a cell phone. "My number's programmed in. If you need anything, call me."

"You didn't have to do that."

"Just promise you'll do what I said."

"I promise."

I grab my laptop bag and head into the main resort building. When I get to the club's entrance, the team's waiting outside the door. After exchanging greetings, we walk into the club. Ismael's sitting at one of the tables. A quick look around tells me he's the only one here.

"Good afternoon, Mr. Anderson. I take it this is your crew?"

"It is. Will your brother be joining us?"

"Unfortunately, he was called away on another matter. I'll be overseeing today's work."

I don't like this at all, but I school my features and instruct my team. "The first camera will be installed at the club's entrance to catch anyone going in or out, and we need several discreet cameras inside the club. The final camera will be installed at the back exit leading to the beach."

The crew wastes no time getting to work. I join Ismael at his table. "The wireless cameras allow for quick and easy installation. Your current system doesn't support security feeds outside the villas. My system will give you the flexibility to have your entire property under constant surveillance. The system runs on encrypted software that is impenetrable."

He nods.

"Your brother said I'd have access to your computer system to set up the software."

Ismael stands. "Yes. Follow me." We exit through a door marked *staff only* and walk down a quiet hallway until we come to the office. "After you."

"May I?" I ask as I motion to the desk.

Ismael again nods and sits on the black leather sofa along the office's back wall. I sit in the oversized leather chair and pull out my laptop to begin transferring the program.

While I work, Ismael pulls out his phone and appears to be texting. Something feels very off about this situation, but I'm too far in to turn back now. There's also the promise I made to Jessica. Failure is not an option. But I've never wished for Dimitri's presence more than I do right now. He can be a pain in the ass, but when it comes to tech skills, there's no one better than him.

Dimitri

"I'M JUST PULLING UP NOW," I SAY TO MAXIM, WHO'S on the phone. "I'll be in touch once I know something."

Strolling into the resort, I make my way to the check-in desk. I'm registered under an assumed name. Just a guy on vacation. Check-in is a breeze. Before I know it, I'm on my way up to the tenth floor to my room. The first thing I do is put the 'do not disturb' sign on the door. Then, I start setting up my equipment. I need to get a good feel for the security system and hack into it as fast as possible. Which isn't hard to do.

The next order of business is to check all the camera feeds and familiarize myself with them. I'm pleasantly surprised to find the cameras have audio capability. So, not only can I see what's going on, but I can also hear it—that gives me another advantage.

The Cinnamon Room has a flurry of activity going on. I watch for a few minutes. It appears new security cameras are being installed—bingo. Three guys are working on the setup, but there's no sign of Viktor. My monitor has all the security camera images running, so I sit back and wait.

A half-hour passes before I spot Viktor walking into the Cinnamon Room with Ismael Hasani on his heels.

"We're all good in here, boss," one of the men says. "We just need to install the camera on the back exit, and we'll be done."

"Excellent work as always," Viktor replies. "I'll be back tonight after the club opens."

"Of course, Mr. Anderson," Ismael says and shakes Viktor's hand. "I'm anticipating seeing your software in action."

Viktor leaves the club with the three men. As soon as he's out the door, Ismael makes a call. I'm hoping to hear who he's calling, but he exits the club through the same staff door. There doesn't appear to be any cameras in that area.

I make a call to give Max a quick update.

"I didn't expect to hear from you already."

"I was able to get right into the existing security system and found Viktor right away. He had a few guys with him that were installing the new system. He was with Ismael Hasani."

"What the hell is Viktor thinking?"

"Apparently, nothing." I continue watching the footage tracking Viktor's movements to the end of the main lobby, but then I lose him. With a couple clicks on my keyboard, I get into the resort's guest log. "I found where he's staying. He's in a private villa. He's expected in the Cinnamon Room tonight. Once I know he's gone, I'll get in his villa and make a copy of his security software."

"Be careful. I don't need the both of you in trouble."

"Careful is my middle name, boss." I laugh as I disconnect the call.

Over the next few hours, I continue to watch the feed. Ismael Hasani makes an appearance moments before the club opens. Viktor enters a few minutes later. The men go back through the staff door.

It's time to make my move.

The sun hasn't yet set, so I put on my cap and sunglasses as I walk through the main lobby at a leisurely pace. I don't want to attract unwanted attention. It's much busier down here now that the club is open. I glance in and see there are several people inside. A relatively small crowd, but it is a Monday. Then, I continue straight out the back exit. One path leads to the resort's private beach, and the other goes to the left, where the villas are located.

"Ginger Villa," I mutter as I walk up to the door. "They really took Grenada's reputation as the spice island to the extreme." Using my phone and the master key card I acquired, I let myself in.

"Viktor?" a feminine voice calls from the bathroom. "Did you forget something?" She comes out with a towel wrapped around her body. "Who are you?" She backs up against the wall.

I put my hands up. "I'm a friend of Viktor's. I won't hurt you."

She looks around the room, her eyes stopping on the cell phone lying on the bed. "Viktor doesn't have any friends here."

"My name's Dimitri. Viktor and I have known each other for years."

"How did you get in here?"

I hold up my phone, showing her the digital keycard.

"Where did you get that?"

"I made it." I shrug.

She moves to take the phone, but I grab her wrist, stopping her.

"We're not going to call anyone."

"Let me go." She struggles to get out of my grasp.

"Relax. I'm not going to hurt you."

"I said, let me go." She pulls out of my grasp, and her towel falls to the floor.

I know I should look away, but I can't. She's fucking gorgeous. The girl scrambles to pick up the towel to cover herself. I take the opportunity to grab the cell that was lying there.

"Why don't you put some clothes on, and then we'll talk?" Although I wouldn't mind talking without her clothes on.

"Give me my phone."

"Nope. Can't do that. Go, get dressed, please."

"Viktor will be back any second. If you don't want to get caught, you better get out of here," she says and spins around, returning to the bathroom.

"Viktor's busy. He won't be back for a while."

She doesn't respond except to slam the bathroom door.

I know I shouldn't be aroused looking at the woman who's with Viktor, but I can't help it. He certainly has good taste. While she's in the bathroom, I open the laptop and start searching. If I get Viktor out of here alive, the first thing we're doing is sitting down to learn about cyber security. Everything I need is in folders on his desktop. I stick my flash drive in, and in a matter of seconds, I have all the info I need. I close the laptop and sit on the bed to wait for the girl. Several minutes later, she comes back in shorts and a T-shirt, this time.

"If Viktor comes back here—"

"I plan to be gone before that. And you aren't going to tell him I'm here."

"Why should I trust you?"

"Because if you don't, Viktor's life could be at stake." I pat the bed next to me. "Let's start by you telling me who you are and why you're here."

She crosses her arms over her chest. "Because Viktor bought me for the week."

"Wrong. Viktor would never buy a woman. Try again."

She blows out a frustrated breath before explaining the story. I can't believe what she's telling me. I thought Viktor was smarter than this.

"He's gotten himself into a real mess." I stand and run my hand through my hair. "I have to figure out how to get Viktor out of here alive."

"Is he in danger?" she asks quietly.

"You and I both know Hasani is not a good man. I think you can answer that question yourself."

"What can I do to help?"

"First, you will not tell Viktor I'm here." I go to the desk and pull open the drawers, searching for paper and pen. "Here's my number. Memorize it and then destroy the paper. If you hear anything important, call me, but make sure you delete the call from the log. Viktor's life depends on this."

"Okay." She takes the paper from my hand.

"Remember, not a word."

She nods.

I leave quickly and head back up to my room. I'm trusting a complete stranger with not only my safety but Viktor's as well. This does not sit well with me.

Viktor

Saimir's been away on business all week. Jessica and I have made a few public appearances to continue the ruse, but other than that, it's been pretty uneventful.

So far, Ismael's impressed with the security system. Tonight's the big test, though. It's Friday night, which means the club will be packed, and Saimir is expected to be back. I'm told we'll be in the main office so I can show Hasani how to operate the software.

I'm hoping I'll come across some information to help me achieve my goal and get Jessica and myself out of here sooner rather than later.

Jessica left a few hours ago to get ready for work. I'm doing everything I can to protect her until I can get her to safety. I'd rather her not be there, but despite all my protests, Hasani insists she works for the club on weekends.

I step outside to get some air, hoping it will quiet my nerves. My phone buzzes with a text.

Mr. Smith: I haven't heard from you all week. I want an update.

Nightingale: The security system is installed. Hasani was away all week. We're meeting tonight.

Mr. Smith: This is taking too long.

Nightingale: You knew this wasn't going to be easy. Hasani doesn't leave much to chance. I'll update you in the morning.

I slide my cell into my pocket and head over to the club.

When I get there, people are already filtering in. Then, right on cue, Hasani comes through the staff door to greet me.

"Are you ready, Mr. Anderson?"

"Everything's run smoothly all week. I'm certain it'll be no different tonight."

"Hopefully, I'll be as impressed as my brother." He motions for me to follow him back to his office. Another young woman is there. "Tell Crystal to come to my office."

"Yes, sir," she says and hurries off.

Why does he want Jessica in the office? The hairs on my neck stand on end.

Once we get settled, I power up the program, explaining how it works to Hasani as I go. The video feed is crystal clear, and the sound quality is studio-perfect.

"My men have attempted to hack into the system several times this week," Hasani announces. "They were unsuccessful every time."

"I told you the software's impenetrable."

There's a knock on the door.

"Come in."

Crystal walks in wearing the tiniest bit of clothes. It leaves little to the imagination. My jaw tenses.

"Do you like the new uniforms, Mr. Anderson?"

"I don't like that she's on display for every man in here when we had a deal." I motion for her to come to me and pull her to my lap.

"No one will touch her, but looking wasn't part of our arrangement." He snickers.

"Consider this a warning if anyone so much as reaches for her. They will meet their end in a most unfortunate way."

Hasani shakes his head. "I think you're becoming too attached to *my* property."

"She's keeping my dick wet and my bed warm, but I assure you, she'll be forgotten once I leave." Jessica glances at me. She has no reason to believe my promise of safety, which is clear from the hurt look in her eyes. I pull her to me and kiss her deeply. "Don't worry, I'm not through with you yet," I try to reassure her.

"You are through for now. Crystal has a special assignment tonight. Room 1003 is requesting personal room service."

I raise my eyebrow.

"Not to worry, Mr. Anderson. She'll only be delivering his meal and any other mundane tasks he requires. Run along now." Hasani watches her until she's out of sight. "She's a hot piece of ass, isn't she?" He looks at me.

"Yes." I clench my fists under the desk.

"Now, where were we?"

I spend the rest of the evening watching the security footage. Hasani's in and out of the office all night. He keeps a strong presence in the club, especially on the weekends. He's pleased with our ability to successfully track the guests as they move about the resort.

The club finally clears out around three a.m. Between being with Hasani and worrying about Jessica, it was an exhausting night. She never returned to the club. I can only hope she's okay.

I'm shutting down my system when the office door opens, and Hasani walks in.

"Well, Mr. Anderson. I'm very pleased with your product."

"As I knew you would be." I lean back in the chair as if I own the space.

Hasani sits on his leather sofa. "I'd like to make you an offer on the original setup we discussed, but I want to expand it. In addition to the cameras we discussed, I want cameras placed on all the floors of the main resort building and in a few of my staff areas."

"That can be arranged for a price."

"No price is too great to ensure I have the safest resort on the island."

"Of course."

"And to celebrate, I'm hosting a party in your honor."

"Oh?"

"I have an exclusive beachfront area reserved for only my most important guests. We'll celebrate our new partnership there tomorrow night."

"That sounds good." I know the area he's referring to. It'll be the perfect place to take out my target while giving me an easy escape. "I'm assuming Crystal will be at my disposal for the party?"

"Of course. I'll have a suitable outfit delivered to your villa for her tomorrow."

I make my way toward the door but stop before I open it. "I found an apartment. This will be my last weekend at the resort."

"We'll be sorry to see you go."

Saimir

"EVERYTHING'S SET FOR TOMORROW NIGHT."
"Yes, sir. We'll be ready."
"Viktor Dobrow has crossed the wrong man."

Viktor

I RETURN TO THE VILLA EXPECTING TO FIND JESSICA, but she isn't there yet. Where the hell is she? We only have tonight to get our shit together. Tomorrow's going to happen fast. She needs to know the plan. There's a knock on the door. When I look, I see it's a guard, and he has Jessica with him. I pull the door open quickly.

"It's about time you returned her."

The guard says nothing and walks away. I close and lock the door.

"Where were you?"

"The guest I had to serve was very demanding."

"Was it a man?"

"Yes. But he didn't hurt me."

"Did he touch you?"

"No." She moves into the room and sits on the bed. "I'm just exhausted."

I sit next to her and take a deep breath. "I'm getting you out of here tomorrow."

"What?"

I relay all the information about tomorrow night. Luck's on my side. This is the perfect opportunity to neutralize Hasani without putting the general population of the resort at risk. It's really a best-case scenario for us.

"I've already reserved a room in the main building. It's a late check-in, so I can skip the desk and go right up to the room." I stand and start pacing. "Hasani's having an outfit sent to the villa for you tomorrow. We'll get ready like we're going to a party so we don't draw attention to ourselves."

"What about all our stuff?" She looks around the room.

"Other than the clothes we're wearing, it's all getting left behind. I'll destroy the laptop before we leave. Once we get to safety, I'll have to call in some favors to get you identification so you can go home."

"Home?"

"You want to go home, right?"

"I don't have a home."

Jessica falls fast asleep, but I lay awake. I'm trying to imagine every way tomorrow might go. Trying to plan for every possible scenario. To consider everything that can go wrong. Before I know it, the sun is shining through the window.

"Good morning," Jessica rolls onto her side and rubs her eyes.

"Hopefully, it's a good morning. Breakfast should be here any minute."

The phone in the room rings.

"Hello?"

"Ah, good morning, Mr. Anderson."

"What can I do for you, Mr. Hasani?"

"Crystal's needed to work today."

"It's a weekday, and she's my date tonight."

"She'll be back in time for the party."

"I had plans for her today."

"Plans?"

"She's a woman. It's a party. I was treating her to a spa day."

Hasani laughs. "Crystal's a paid escort. A whore. She's not entitled to a *spa* day."

"While she's with me, she's entitled to whatever I choose to give her."

"That's where you're wrong, Mr. Anderson. Crystal remains my employee, and she'll do only what I allow. And today, she *will* be working. Make sure she's at the Cinnamon Room in ten minutes."

"We're just getting out of bed. She'll be there after we eat."

"Perhaps I haven't made myself clear. This is my resort, and Crystal is my property. It is I who calls the shots."

"We haven't signed the contract for the security system yet." I make the unspoken threat. "She eats before she leaves my room. And she'll return no later than five to have time to properly prepare for tonight. It's my arm she'll be on, and I expect a certain level of presentation from any woman with me."

"I'll make a concession this time."

"Good day, Mr. Hasani." I hang up the phone.

"Do you have a death wish?" Jessica asks.

"Why?"

"No one talks to him that way."

"I've dealt with much worse than him. He doesn't realize it, but his time on the earth is rapidly coming to an end."

Breakfast is delivered a short time later. We discuss the specifics of what will happen tonight while we eat.

Then, with much reluctance, I watch her leave the villa.

Dimitri

I put in a special request and a substantial sum of money to ensure Jessica's available whenever I call for her services. I spend the better part of the day watching and listening. Hasani's setting up for a party in his private outdoor venue. Other than that, things have been quiet. I purposely haven't requested Jessica's services, hoping that if she's hanging around with the staff and Hasani, she'll overhear something. It isn't until lunchtime I request she deliver my food and stay to tidy my room —it'll give us some time to talk.

While I wait for her arrival, Hasani shows up outside the Cinnamon Room. He's met by several other men who follow him inside. I sit up in my seat. "What's going on here?"

"Gentlemen, good to see you," Hasani says.

"Is everything set for tonight?" one of the men asks.

"My people are setting up the venue now." He motions outside. "I'll make sure you have access to my penthouse. When I call Dobrow onto the stage to introduce him, you'll have a clear shot," Hasani explains.

"What the fuck?" His cover's blown. There's a knock on my door. "Shit." I throw the door open quickly, knowing it'll be Jessica. "Hurry up and come over here."

"What's wrong?" she asks.

"Viktor's cover is blown." I point to the screen.

Jessica sits next to me while we continue to listen. The men are highly armed with sniper rifles and have a solid plan.

"Do you recognize any of these men?"

She points to the screen. "That's the man who brought me here."

The blood coursing through my body boils with rage.

The other men have their backs to the camera, making identifying them impossible. They talk for a few more minutes before going their separate ways, presumably to set up in Hasani's penthouse—where there are no cameras.

"Viktor's planning to kill Hansani tonight," Jessica says.

"What did he tell you?"

Jessica details everything Viktor told her. There's no way my friend is going to pull this off by himself. Hell, I don't know if either of us will make it out of here.

"Shit." I stand and start pacing. "Why the hell did he do this?"

Jessica stands and touches my arm, stilling me. "What do we do?"

"We? *We* aren't going to do anything. I'll handle this."

This girl is half my size but places her hands on her hips and stands up to me anyway. She's hot as hell, spunky, and intelligent. Why does Viktor get all the good women?

"Yes, I am. There's no way you're doing this without me, Dimitri."

I turn away from her. The last thing I want to do is include this girl in my plans. We're severely outnumbered, and the Albanians are crazy as fuck. If anything happens to Viktor's girl, he'll kill me. Our chances of getting out of this alive are getting smaller by the second. But I don't think I have another choice. I need her help. Turning back to face her, I ask, "If I could just contact Viktor. Do you have your cell on you?" It's time he finds out I'm here.

"No. It's too risky during the day. But I know his number."

I punch in his cell number, and it starts ringing. "Come on, Viktor. Pick up." I have to try to talk some sense into him. But the line just rings and rings. "He doesn't have voicemail set up?" I look to Jessica.

"I don't know. I haven't had to call him."

What do I do now? Think Dimitri. I can't go to his villa, and I can't ask Jessica to tell him I'm here—it's too risky. "I'm going to have to take out the sniper before they take him out. Here's what I need you to do."

I send Jessica on her way with my instructions. Then, I go back to watching the video feed. I hope to get some clues as to where Viktor is and how I can try fixing this mess he's made.

While I watch, I call Max.

"They know who he is. Hasani is planning on taking him out at a party tonight, and Viktor has some crazy plan that's going to get him killed."

"Where the hell is his head?"

"Somewhere back in New York City, I suspect." Do I tell him? What the hell? "It appears that he's moving on. He's had a girl on his arm the whole time I've been here. She works for Hasani. I had to ask for her help."

"Do you trust her?"

"Hasani stole her. She's very much into Viktor. Yes, I trust her." I have no choice but to trust her. I run my hands through my hair. "Boss, I have no idea how I'm going to get us out of here."

"I'll do everything I can from here."

"If we're still alive in a few hours, I'll be in touch."

Viktor

I'VE SPENT THE AFTERNOON CHANGING MY APPEARANCE. Gone is the hair I've spent the past year or so growing out. And no more contacts. When I look in the mirror, my reflection is once again familiar.

Using my burner phone, I make a last-minute reservation for an ocean-front room with a balcony on one of the top floors of the resort. It's off-season for this area, so getting a room was easy. The rooms in the main resort building use a phone app to open the room doors, so I don't have to worry about checking in. The room's placement will give me an unobstructed shot at Hasani.

It's five o'clock, and she's not here. Her dress arrived hours ago. I pace back and forth, hoping she shows up soon. Another hour passes, and still nothing. The party starts at seven. The phone in my room rings.

"Hello?"

"Mr. Anderson, it's Crystal."

"Where are you?"

"Something's come up, and I'm not going to be able to attend tonight's function with you," she says quietly.

"What are you talking about? Is it Hasani?"

"No, sir."

"What's going on?"

"It was a pleasure serving you, Mr. Anderson. I hope you have a lovely evening." She hangs up.

Immediately I dial the number to Hasani's office.

"Why the hell did Crystal call me and back out of tonight?"

"I wasn't aware she did."

"We just hung up. Her refusal is unacceptable. I expect her at my door in ten minutes."

"Mr. Anderson, perhaps she doesn't appreciate a man as *forceful* as yourself."

"Ten minutes or the deal's off." I slam the phone down.

Ten minutes pass, and no Jessica. I don't know what to do. Hasani is going to be dead within the hour. After I fire the shot, I won't have time to look for her. This place will be crawling with Hasani's men. If I make it out alive, it'll be a miracle, but I promised Jessica she'd get out of here. How am I supposed to make good on that if she's not here?

I wait as long as possible, but she never shows. "Fuck, Jessica. Why did you do this?" I double-check my weapon, then grab my tactical bag. It's now or never.

When I step outside, there's a thick cloud cover obstructing the moonlight. Finally, something's working in my favor. I can leave my villa and get to the beach, where I walk away from the resort. I keep walking past several other resorts before going through a parking lot, where I backtrack my steps.

Once I'm back at Hasani's resort, I walk through the main doors like every other guest and head straight to the elevators. The hallway to my room is quiet. As soon as I get in the room, I lock the door and try the phone I gave Jessica once more, but there's no answer. "Dammit." There's no time to waste. I have to get myself set up before they realize Mr. Anderson isn't showing up.

Saimir

Viktor thought he'd outsmart us by using an alias and shaving his head. Well, he was wrong. Clearly, he has a death wish. Tonight, I'll be his genie in a bottle—his wish is my command.

"There's been a change of plans," I say to my sniper. "Dobrow is in 1417. Keep one man in the penthouse, just in case. Then, adjust your position on the beach. It'll be a clear shot to the balcony of his room."

"Yes, sir. I'm on it."

Dimitri

THERE'S A KNOCK ON MY DOOR. JESSICA'S RIGHT ON time. Pulling the door open, I let Jessica in.

"We don't have much time," she says as she pushes past me.

"I know. I heard."

Viktor thought he could outsmart the Albanians by shaving his head and using a fake name. He's better than this. Now, I'm left to try to fix this mess without getting the three of us killed.

Jessica's already at the computer. When she demanded she be allowed to help, I had no idea she studied computer programming before being kidnapped. Jessica was in Paris doing an exchange student program. She has some wicked skills that she's acquired along the way—skills that are very useful right now.

"Saimir's assuming Viktor will be on the balcony of the room he booked. He's got men at the Penthouse and one on the beach." She points to the picture on the security feed. "He blends in with the rest of his security," she says and looks at me. "But I'm familiar with him. He's Saimir's best sniper."

"Fuck." I slam my fists on the desk, making Jessica jump. "I'm sorry. I didn't mean to scare you."

"We're not getting out of here, are we?" A tear drips down her cheek.

"Look at me." I cup her face in my palms and wipe her tears. "I'm getting us all out of here tonight."

Although she nods in agreement, her eyes tell a different story.

"Here's how this is going to happen," I explain the plan quickly while I grab my handgun and holster it on my side. Then, I grab the rifle from my bag.

"How did you get that on a plane?"

"I took a private jet to Venezuela and then a chartered plane here," I say while I work. "We don't have much time." The words no sooner leave my mouth when loud music begins to play.

"They're starting."

I stop in front of Jessica. "Are you ready?"

"Yes."

I pull on my night vision goggles and take a covered position by the balcony doors. I have the perfect view. Now, I just need to wait for a clear shot at the sniper.

A shot rings out. As I pull the trigger, a second shot sounds. I hit my target, and he falls to the ground.

"Now," I yell to Jessica.

Screams come from the beach, and then the resort goes black.

"Come on." I grab her arm and pull her along through the pitch-black hallway and into the stairwell. I push the rifle into her hand. "Stay right here, and don't make a sound."

I take the steps three at a time, racing to the fourteenth floor. Viktor's room is six doors from the stairwell. The sniper got a shot out a split second before mine hit him. I'm not sure what I'm going to find when I get into his room.

Thankfully, the resort employees still use old-fashioned keys to access the guests' rooms. Jessica often works in housekeeping and managed to slip a key out. I slide it into the lock and turn it. With a click, the door opens.

I run to the balcony and find Viktor on the ground, propped against the wall.

"Fuck. How bad is it?"

"Dimitri? What the hell are you doing here?"

"Saving your sorry ass. Where are you hit?"

"My shoulder."

He has his hand over the spot where he was hit. Blood pours from his hand.

"Can you walk?"

"I think so."

He leans his weight on me as I help him up. I peer out over the balcony rail. There's a flurry of activity down on the beach. Hasani's men are everywhere.

"We don't have much time," I tell him as we head for the door.

"I can't go. I have to find—"

"Jessica, I know. She's in the stairwell waiting for us."

"How did you—"

"I'll fill you in after we get out of here."

Viktor keeps up with me as we hurry down the steps until we meet back up with Jessica.

"He's shot. But we have to hurry. Grab my cell out of my pocket and use it for light."

"Oh my God. How bad is it?" She asks as she slides her tiny hand into my pocket, grabbing my phone.

"It hurts like hell," Viktor growls and takes the rifle from her.

"Let's go. We don't have time for this." The three of us hurry down the steps. Viktor's body is getting heavier as he trips his way down.

Finally, we arrive at the side emergency exit door. I push it open, not knowing what we'll find on the other side. I take a small breath when there's no one there.

"Come on. We're almost there." I see our ride waiting at the other end of the parking lot.

We're halfway across when the resort's lights go back on.

"There he is," a voice calls behind us, followed by a shot. I push Jessica down behind a car and pull out my pistol, firing a shot back.

"Jessica, run to the black car and don't look back. I'll cover you from here."

"I'm not leaving you two behind."

"Dammit, Jessica, do as he says," Viktor yells.

"When you get to the car, I want you to close the door and stay down.

With a last look, she takes off for the car. A shot is fired from behind us. It misses by a fraction of an inch, hitting the car next to us. Again, I fire back.

"I need you to run."

"I'm going to slow you down. Just leave me here."

"I'm not leaving you behind."

"Make sure Jessica is safe." He tries to pull away from me, but I don't loosen my grasp on him.

"Shut the fuck up and run." I drag him with me, firing behind us as we run.

Several more shots sound. Bullets ricochet around us. We're almost to the car when a bullet grazes my arm. "Shit."

"Are you hit?"

I pull the door open and shove Viktor into the backseat. "Go," I tell the driver as I jump into the car, avoiding more shots. Before I get the door closed, the driver's already peeling out.

"Now what?" Viktor asks.

"We need to slow this bleeding down." I pull my shirt off and use it as a compress over his wound. He's lost a lot of blood and is starting to look pale. "Maxim has a chartered plane waiting for us."

"Do you have my phone?"

"Mhm." She pulls my phone from her pocket and passes it to me.

"Keep pressure on this." Viktor winces in pain when we hit a bump.

I pull up Maxim's contact and tap the green call button. It rings several times before the call connects.

"Are you out?"

"We're on our way to the airport." I look over at Viktor, whose head is laid back on the seat. "He's been shot." I lower my voice. "He's lost a lot of blood, boss."

"I have some contacts in South America. I will arrange for medical to meet you at the jet."

"Thanks, boss."

"I would like to talk to him."

I hold the phone out to Viktor. "The boss wants to speak to you." Viktor shakes his head. "He doesn't want to talk."

Maxim's silent. He's not a man you say no to. I brace myself for the worst, but he surprises me. "How bad is he?"

"I'm not a doctor, but I don't like what I see." The driver pulls into the small airport bringing us to where our charter waits. "We just got to the plane." I was so wrapped up in the conversation I didn't realize we were being followed. "We're in trouble."

"What's wrong?"

"Hasani's men are here." The words barely leave my lips when two police cars block their path. "What the hell's going on?"

"I have ensured safe passage out of the country."

I watch as the men get out of their cars. They look to be arguing with the police, who've now drawn their weapons.

"How?" I shouldn't be shocked, but I am.

"Call me when you are on my jet." Max ends the call.

"Are you two ready to get out of here?"

Viktor

I LEAN HEAVILY ON DIMITRI AS WE WALK UP THE STEPS to get into the small jet. The concerned look he and Jessica exchange doesn't escape me.

"Get your ass in a seat." Dimitri tries to keep his fear out of his voice, but I see right through him.

"Make sure she's safe," I whisper.

"You're going to have to do that yourself." He buckles me in as we start to taxi down the runway. Then, he turns to Jessica. "Are you buckled in?"

"Yes"

I feel the plane's wheels leave the ground. The pressure from our ascent increases the pain in my shoulder. My entire body begins to shake from the intensity, and blackness creeps into my peripheral vision.

"Try to take some deep breaths," Dimitri coaches me.

My mind immediately goes back to Natalie in labor with Rose. Except it was me doing the coaching while she was bringing a miracle into the world. The pain in my heart is riveling the pain in my shoulder—God, I miss that woman.

Dimitri

FINALLY, THE PLANE REACHES CRUISING ALTITUDE, AND I throw off my seatbelt. "Jessica, will you grab the medical kit out of my pack and pass me the scissors?" I'm not a doctor or anything, but in my line of work, we're used to patching up a gunshot wound until we can get real medical help. "I need to take your shirt off so I can get a good look at this."

"Leave it be." Viktor swipes my hand away.

"Do you want to bleed to death?"

"It doesn't matter."

It doesn't matter? Does he want to die? Then it hits me. Yes, he does. Losing Natalie and the kid really screwed him up. He doesn't care if he lives or dies. Well, he's not dying on my watch. "Shut the fuck up and let me get this shirt off."

Viktor rests his head back while I make quick work of cutting his shirt open. Jessica helps me remove it. The blood oozing from the open wound doesn't even cause her to flinch.

"What do we do?" she asks.

"We're going to clean it up." Holding Viktor's arm, I pull him forward. "Let me see the back." He rolls his eyes, but he lets me move him. "Well, the good news is the bullet is not lodged in your shoulder. The bad news is the back looks worse than the front."

I get up and begin rummaging through my medical kit. Jessica comes over and stands next to me.

"He doesn't look so good," she whispers. "How long until we get to Venezuela?"

"Too long." I look over at my friend. The color is drained from his face, and he's shivering. He's going into shock. "I'm going to attempt to stitch him up. It'll at least stop the blood loss."

"Is he going to make it?" Her eyes fill with tears.

"I won't let him die."

Viktor's been like a brother to me since we were eighteen. We had each other's backs while we served in the military and all the years we've worked for Max. I'll be damned if I lose him now.

"Natalie," Viktor's voice cracks. "Where are you? I need to feel you." His arm reaches out.

I look at Jessica, startled. Hearing Viktor call out for the woman he was in love with in front of his new fling isn't going to go over well. "I'm sure he didn't mean to call for her."

"It's okay. He told me the whole story."

"He did?" Jessica doesn't appear phased. Instead, she looks at him with compassion.

"Natalie," he calls out again.

This time, Jessica goes over. "Feel me." She takes his hand in hers. "I'm right here."

"Hey, buddy," I say, lowering in front of him. "I'm gonna give you a shot of something to try to numb this. But I'm not going to lie. This is going to hurt."

Jessica holds his hand while I do my best to stitch his skin closed. At this point, I'm just trying to stop the bleeding. I wish he'd wince or yell, but his body fell slack when he passed out a few minutes ago.

"Hold on, Vik," I beg. "Don't die on me."

Viktor

I CALL FOR NATALIE, AND SHE COMES TO ME. I thought I'd lost her, but it must've been a dream because she's in my arms. Her hand caresses my face as she whispers to me. "I love you so much," I say. "And I love our baby, Rose." I may not have helped create her, but that little girl owns my heart. The three of us are a family—they're all I have.

But then she floats away. Coldness replaces the warmth of her presence.

I'm alone again.

I hear voices around me, but not the one voice I want to hear. I recognize the words spoken in Russian. The deep timbre's familiar, but I have to search the recess of my mind for its owner.

Maxim.

Where am I?

Slowly, I open my eyes. It takes several minutes before things come into focus and for me to figure out where I am. I attempt to sit up, but the searing pain in my shoulder forces me back down.

"Oh my God, Viktor. You're finally awake," Lana says.

"H-how did—" My throat is dry, making it hard to speak.

"You gave us quite a scare," Maxim adds. "It is nice to have you back."

"What am I doing here?" I ask and try to sit up again, but Max's strong arm stops me.

"Relax. Dimitri brought you back to us. Kazimir, my personal physician, had a heck of a time stitching you back together." Once I lay back down, he sits in his chair. "You lost a lot of blood and then developed an infection. It was touch and go for a bit."

"How long have I been out?"

"Almost two weeks," Lana says. "I'll be right back. There's someone who's been waiting for you to wake up."

I wait until Lana leaves the room. "Is she going to get Natalie?"

"Natalie is in New York. With Alex," Max says.

"She can't be. She was on the plane. I felt her. Heard her."

"You must have been dreaming. There was a girl on the plane. Your girlfriend, Jessica."

"Jessica?" The name sounds strangely familiar, but I'm not sure why. "My girlfriend? Everything's fuzzy. All jumbled together."

"Do not worry. Everything will come back to you now that you are awake." Max pats my arm. "I am sure once you see her, you will remember. She is a tenacious little thing." He chuckles.

"Viktor," a petite brunette says my name as she rushes over to my side. "You scared the shit out of us."

"It's about time you woke your lazy ass up," Dimitri says from the doorway.

I stare at the young woman at my side. She takes my hand in hers, but it feels wrong, and I pull away.

"I'm sorry," she says, folding her hands in her lap.

"We will leave you two to talk." Max walks toward the door. "Let us go, Dimitri."

"Right behind you, boss. Welcome back, brother."

I nod as I return my gaze back to the girl.

"Do you know who I am?" she asks quietly.

I search her face, looking for clues. Struggling to mix the familiarity of her face with my lack of knowledge. A switch flips.

It's like a movie begins to play on fast-forward. I'm in Grenada. She's in my room. The dress. The party. The plane. "Jessica."

She smiles. "You remember me."

"You were supposed to come back to my room, but you called and said no."

"I did." She looks down at her hands. "Can I explain?"

"Please do."

She tells me how she met Dimitri and how they worked together. "I couldn't come to you because Dimitri needed my help."

Her eyes sparkle when she says his name. "Do you and Dimitri have something going on?"

She shakes her head. "He's barely said two words to me since we got here. This place is incredible, by the way."

"I don't remember you being so relaxed."

"Well." She looks around. "It's safe here."

"Did you call your family?"

"Yes."

"I'm sure they were relieved to hear from you." Carefully, I try to sit up but groan in pain. Jessica helps me and props pillows behind my back.

"I guess." She shrugs.

"That doesn't sound very positive." From having worked with Maxim for so long, I know not every family is overjoyed that their loved one has been found.

"Things are complicated with my parents, to say the least. I won't be going back to the States." She moves from the edge of the bed to the chair. "Irina brought me to Jelena's Hope to talk to a therapist. They're helping me deal with everything. And Irina said they'll help me start a new life wherever I want. I want to stay here. If everything works out."

For some reason, I sense there's much more to her story than she's telling me, but I won't push. When she's ready, if she's ready, she'll open up. Unfortunately, I'm starting to get tired already, and as hard as I try to hide it, a yawn escapes.

"You should get some rest. I'm glad you're going to be okay." Jessica heads for the door. She reaches for the doorknob but stops herself. Then, turning around, she asks, "Can you do me a favor?"

"I'll try."

"Can you tell Dimitri that you and I aren't together?"

I laugh. "Yeah. I think I can manage that."

Viktor

I can't believe I lost two weeks of my life. Two weeks that Hasani has continued to roam the earth. As soon as I get back to normal, I'm heading back to finish what I started.

Kasimir has come to check on me several times. The infection is finally cleared up, and my stitches are out. I have strengthening exercises to do every day to hopefully gain back the muscle tone I've lost. The most concerning thing is the residual numbness in my hand. The doc doesn't have an answer for me. It's a wait-and-see-what-happens kind of deal.

Meanwhile, I'm an animal stuck in a cage. Every move I make is done so under a microscope. Irina tells me it's for my own good, so I make a full recovery. Max has been quiet. Other than telling me Lady Clare's being cared for at Jelena's Hope, he refuses to discuss anything work-related.

I haven't seen much of Lana. Jessica said they are getting along really well, but I know Lana. She's usually the social butterfly bouncing from place to place. But since I've been here, she's been getting more reclusive.

I've just finished my physiotherapy in Max's gym. I'm heading to the indoor pool to swim a few laps before tonight's festivities. Amelia graduated secondary school last week. That kid's come a long way since we recovered her from Moreno's. She seems to be thriving as part of the Solonik family.

Last night, we all attended the traditional Last Bell ceremony and dance. It's an old Soviet-era tradition that, for some reason, lives on. The graduating class works diligently on perfecting a waltz that's performed for all the parents. Afterward, they pair up with an incoming first grader to plant Birch Trees. It's almost like a rite of passage for the graduate and the little one. Tonight, she's having a more American-style graduation party. The house will be crawling with teens. I plan on being in my room with the door locked long before that chaos ensues.

When I step into the pool room, I freeze. Amelia's sitting on a wicker chair, her laptop on the table in front of her. Natalie's image is on the screen. The two are deep in conversation and haven't noticed me walk in. I stay quiet for a few minutes, savoring the sound of Natalie's voice before clearing my throat to make my presence known.

"I didn't hear you come in. I'm sorry," Amelia says quickly as she looks back and forth between Natalie and me. "I can— Umm — I'll go somewhere else." She moves to pick up her laptop.

"No, stay here. It's okay." I can't take my eyes off the screen. "Natalie. How are you?"

"I'm doing well." Her smile lights up her face. "I'm glad to see you up and around. You gave us all a good scare."

"It's been a rough few weeks, I guess."

I can't take my eyes off her. My brain urges me to tell her everything that's happened, but my mouth refuses to utter a sound.

"Mama. Mama," Rose calls and toddles over.

Her sweet face is almost my undoing.

"Auntie Melia," she says. Then, her eyes open wide. "Frickter?"

She remembers me. I have to swallow over the lump in my throat. "Printessa, you've gotten so big."

"You come see me?"

"Frickter is at *Dedushka*'s house very far away. He can't come see you right now," Natalie explains.

"Oh." Her earlier smile is replaced with a frown. She pushes her bottom lip out just like she did when she was a baby.

She's grown so much this past year. Her blonde curls hang down to her shoulders like her mama's. Her big brown eyes are so expressive. They tell a story all their own. And those chubby pink cheeks. I remember how soft they were when I used to kiss her tiny face.

"Natalie, are you and Amelia still on the phone?" Alex asks as he comes into view of the camera. "Viktor." He looks surprised to see me. "We heard you were back. It's good to see you."

"You too." I have to get out of here. Now. The wounds I thought were healed are bursting open, threatening to pour out. "I forgot something I promised to do for Max. It was nice talking to you." I turn to leave.

"*Ya lyublyu tyebya,* Frickter," Rose says.

Her tiny voice nearly brings me to my knees. I close my eyes and try to push down the grief that's trying to claw its way to the surface. I can't speak. Can't turn back to the camera. So, I do the only thing I can manage. I walk away.

"I'm sorry, Viktor," Amelia calls.

I nod and get out of the room as fast as I can. I don't stop until I'm back in my bedroom. I lock the door and lean up against it to catch my breath. I can no longer hold back the tears that are wetting my face. My falling apart is something I don't want anyone else to witness. Although it's been over a year, seeing them brought back the pain as though it were just yesterday.

I should be happy they're together and well, but instead, I still wish it was me by her side. What the hell is wrong with me?

Maxim

"My daughter, this beautiful young lady, has brought much joy into our family," I begin my toast in Amelia's honor. "And today we celebrate the completion of her secondary education as well as her being honored with the Outstanding Academic Success Gold Medal Award." Our guests applaud.

"Dad," she whispers, her cheeks pink.

Amelia is not comfortable being the center of attention, but right now, she deserves praise for every accolade she has earned. She has been through things no young woman, no person should ever have to face. Yet, she has come through it as a strong and self-confident young lady.

"Many of you know that Amelia is an accomplished pianist. Something first instilled in her by her biological family." I put my hand on her shoulder, knowing she often gets emotional talking about her parents. "Irina and I have been honored to be able to stand in for them and finish the job they began. Much to my dismay," I pause. "Amelia has decided to attend university in California to study music." Our guests laugh. I am certain remembering a very similar speech when Svetlana was going off to New York City. "Obviously, neither of my girls takes pity on their father's nerves."

"Look at it as a growing experience, Papa," Lana says and smiles.

"Irina and I will miss her very much, but we could not be any more proud of her accomplishments, and we cannot wait to see what the future holds for her." I raise my glass of champagne. "To Amelia and her future success."

The clink of glasses sounds around us as our guests toast my daughter. Then, the real party begins. Food is being served, and a DJ starts playing popular music—the kind the kids like. Irina and I make our way to the adult side of the party, away from the music and the splashing of teenagers in the outdoor pool.

I notice Viktor with the security team. "Excuse me, please," I say to the guests we are sitting with and go over to Viktor. "You are not working tonight. You are our guest. Come sit with us."

"Come on, boss. I'm fine to work."

"We will discuss your return to work tomorrow. Tonight, you will join us as a guest."

He rolls his eyes but follows me over to where we are sitting. As the evening progresses, he never lets his guard down. Never stops scanning for possible threats.

But when I look into his eyes, I see he is still lost. Amelia told Irina and me what happened earlier when he walked in on her conversation with Natalie. Even though a year has passed, his heart has not moved on.

When he arrived with Jessica, I thought perhaps there was a spark there. After observing them together, they function more like a brother and sister. The real spark is between Jessica and Dimitri. I am glad for him, but that does nothing to stop my concern about Viktor.

"I'm feeling pretty worn out," Viktor says. "I think I'm going to turn in early."

"Are you sure?"

"Yeah. It's been a long day." Then, without any further conversation, he walks away.

"He's still in a bad place, Max," Irina says. "I'm worried about him."

"As am I."

Viktor

Max invited me as a guest at Amelia's graduation party, but it feels wrong. I should be working security with the other guys. I feel useless. This afternoon didn't help. I'm still feeling the effects of seeing Natalie and Rose on the video call. The darkness of depression is beckoning me to come back and drown in its depths.

Despite being outside, everything begins to close in around me, and I quickly excuse myself from the party. On my way into the house, I stop by where Amelia is talking to a small group of girls.

"Congratulations on your graduation."

"Thank you," she says quietly.

Her friends giggle like little schoolgirls. Amelia rolls her eyes at their reaction.

"Are you leaving already?"

"I'm pretty tired. I guess I'm still recovering." I shrug and turn to walk away.

"Viktor." Amelia touches my arm. "I'm sorry about earlier. I didn't mean—"

"There's nothing to apologize for. Enjoy your party."

As I walk away, the girls continue to giggle and whisper loudly to Amelia about me. One of them wants her to ask me if I'd be interested in going out with them.

Can you even imagine? They're barely eighteen-year-old children.

On my way back to my room, I pass Lana's room.

"You ditched the party early, too?" she asks when she sees me.

"Parties aren't my thing." I lean against her doorway. "Why aren't you out there? You're usually the life of the party."

"I don't feel much like socializing tonight."

"Just tonight?"

She shrugs.

"Why did you drop everything and come back here?"

"What do you mean? Why wouldn't I come back *home*?"

I don't miss her emphasis on the word 'home.' "You ditched everything and everyone. When Natalie's life fell apart, her best friend was nowhere to be found."

"She had you. She was fine."

I walk into the room and close the door so we don't attract unwanted attention. "She was fine. Is that what you think?"

"I know she was grieving, but it wasn't like she was alone. You were there with her. She didn't need me."

"Cut the shit, Lana."

She jumps up from where she's sitting on her bed. "Everyone's always worried about poor Natalie. Her husband died. Oh wait, you stepped right in and warmed her bed. She had a baby. You took the place of her father. Natalie had everything," she yells. "Did it ever occur to anyone that maybe not all of us are as lucky as Natalie?"

"Lucky?" I spit the word back at her. "Losing your husband, the father of your unborn baby, is such great luck. Maybe it's best you left. What kind of fucking friend is jealous of a grieving widow?"

Lana looks like someone's punched her in the gut. "I'm sorry. I didn't mean what I said." She sits on the edge of her bed. "I was going through my own shit. I would've only made things worse for everyone."

"Look, I know we're not close, but I'm here, and I can listen."

"It's in the past. That's where I'd like to leave it."

"What about Brandon?" The guy is lost and confused.

"He's better off without me."

"I guess that's your answer for everything."

"Let it go, please, Viktor."

"As you wish." I turn and walk out of her room with no more answers than when I went in. Clearly, she's not okay, but I'm not going to beg. If she wants to put up walls and shut everyone out, that's her problem. I've got enough of my own.

Viktor

I HAVE TO SPEAK TO MAX, BUT I DIDN'T WANT TO bother him too early today. The party went on well into the night.

When I get to his office, the door is open.

"May I come in?"

"Yes," Max answers and sets aside whatever he's working on. "Is everything okay?"

I sink into the leather chair across from his desk. "Kasimir said I'm fully recovered. I want to go back to work. I have a job to finish."

Max rests his elbows on his desk and steeples his fingers. "That is going to be a bit of a problem."

"Oh?" I raise an eyebrow.

"It seems your shot hit Saimir Hasani in the chest. You narrowly missed his heart."

Dammit, I thought I killed the guy.

"Hasani's clan is out for blood."

"I figured as much." I shrug. "I'm going back to finish the job."

"Like hell you are."

"I was paid for the job. I need to see it through."

"I already took care of Mr. Smith. His money was refunded."

"How did you get that information?"

"Dimitri got into your system." Max laughs. "Your tech skills are lacking."

"I have a reputation to protect. I have to go back—"

"You are not going back." Maxim slams his fist on his desk.

I've rarely witnessed Max lose his temper. Anytime he did, it was never good for the man on the receiving end.

"You have no idea the concessions I have made to guarantee your safety—to spare your life." He stands and rounds his desk. "Going off on your own was reckless and sloppy. You had no one to watch your back."

What he's saying makes sense, but even as he says it, I feel nothing. It would've been okay if they killed me. I have nobody to live for.

"Viktor." Max's raised voice startles me. "Did you hear me?"

"Yes. I screwed up."

"That is all you heard?"

I shrug.

"Hasani put a price on your head. The two weeks you were unconscious, I spent not only worrying if you would ever wake up, but I was also bargaining for life in case you did." Max crosses his arms across his broad chest. "Reluctantly, and for a large payout, Hasani handed over the girls. He agreed to stay out of trafficking and to let you live as long as I arranged for a safe channel to transfer weapons—a more lucrative venture of his."

"You shouldn't have done that. My life isn't worth it."

"Enough." Max slices his hand through the air. "I know losing Natalie was hard."

"Hard?" I let out a sarcastic laugh. "She and Rose were everything to me. And just like that, they were gone." I walk over to the wall of windows that overlooks the front of Maxim's property.

"Her rightful place is with Alex," Max softens his voice. "What happened to both you and Alex was an unimaginable tragedy. You put your heart on the line, and it was broken. But you must make peace with it to move forward."

I turn my back on Max and place my hand on the window. "Move forward?"

"I think you should talk to one of the therapists at Jelena's Hope."

"I don't think so."

"Viktor," Max says and moves to stand next to me. "You are not alone. There are people who care about you—including Natalia and Rose. Do you think she would not care if something happened to you? That it would not break her heart?"

I've been a selfish prick. I never stopped to think about how she'd feel. The only person I've considered in all this is me.

"I was there and saw you two together. After you were shot, she called every day to check on your condition. Natalia loves you. A part of her heart will always belong to you. She knows that, and so does Alex—and he accepts that. He misses your friendship." Max puts his hand on my shoulder. "Natalia is just starting to be okay. If something happened to you, it would be more than she could endure."

"I don't know how to do this." I drop my forehead to the glass. "Everyone I've ever loved is gone. I have no one left, Max. Why? Why does everyone I love leave?"

"Talk to one of our therapists. If you cannot do it for yourself, do it for Natalia and Rose. Once they clear you, we can discuss a new assignment—far away from Hasani."

"I promise I'll go once, but there are no guarantees after that."

Viktor

I've had several sessions with Grigor, one of the male therapists at Jelena's Hope. The first few sessions were uncomfortable. We spent most of our time staring at one another. I'm not big on talking about my feelings or getting all touchy-feely. Grigor didn't force me to speak, but he also wasn't going to let me off the hook. He kept scheduling the next session.

Eventually, I gave in. It wasn't much to start with, but Grigor was patient and allowed me to wade through the muddy waters at my own pace.

I guess it's helping. I didn't want to feel anymore. Numbness was easier. But little by little, the numbness I've been living with has been dissipating, giving way to the emotions I was afraid to feel.

We've explored them, one at a time. The abandonment I've struggled with since my parents' deaths. Losing babusya. And most importantly, losing Natalie and Rose. I still don't know that I agree with Grigor that *I'm* not the problem, but I no longer wish myself dead. I've taken a step back and realized the effect it would have on the people around me.

I'm leaving Grigor's office when I see Amelia sitting in the waiting room, playing on her phone.

"What are you doing here?"

"Dad got called back home on business. He asked me to wait and get a ride home with you?"

"Where's Irina?"

"She's out of town with Lana and Jessica, remember?" Amelia stands up. "Are you ready to go?"

"I came on my bike."

A few days after I woke up, I knew it was time to sell my apartment in Belgorod. I put it on the market and had my bike shipped up here.

"Oh." She looks around. "Dad told me you'd bring me home. He's in an important meeting and told me I could only leave with you."

Max might kill me for this. "Are you comfortable with riding on the back of my bike?"

"Sure." Her face lights up. "I think it'll be fun."

Fun. That's what I was thinking, too. My boss's eighteen-year-old daughter, who he's massively overprotective about, is riding on the back of my bike. Sounds like a recipe for disaster to me, but I can't leave her here.

She follows me outside, and I hand her my black leather jacket. "Put this on."

"It's kinda hot for this, don't you think?"

"The heat doesn't matter. It's to protect your arms." I really wish she had pants and proper shoes on instead of shorts and strappy sandals. "It's going to be big, but it'll suit its purpose." I hold the worn jacket up, and she slips her arms into it.

I grab the helmet while she fiddles with the sleeves.

"Put this on too."

"What are you going to wear?"

"I'll be fine."

I help her guide the helmet on and buckle it, making sure it's a snug fit.

"It's really heavy," she complains.

I flick the visor down. "But your head will stay intact if it comes in contact with the ground."

"You're as bad as my father." She giggles.

I ignore her comment and throw my leg over the bike. "Get on behind me."

She easily climbs on. It's an odd feeling. I've never had a girl on my bike.

"You don't need to do anything except hold onto my waist."

"I think I can manage that."

I start up the bike. The engine rumbles beneath us, and then we're on our way. I stick to the speed limit and take as many side roads as possible. The last thing I need is to injure the boss's daughter.

Twenty minutes later, we're pulling up in front of Max's home. Amelia jumps off the bike, pulling the helmet off. She's smiling from ear to ear.

"That was amazing. Can we do that again sometime?"

"I don't think—"

The front door flies open, and Maxim rushes out. "What the hell do you think you are doing?"

"What's wrong?" Amelia asks.

"What is wrong?" He motions to the bike. "What were you thinking putting her on your bike? She could have been killed."

Maxim's level of protectiveness, where his daughters are concerned, is borderline obsessive. If it were up to him, he'd lock them in a tower and never let them out.

"Amelia told me she needed a ride home. I took my bike to the center. There wasn't much choice." I take the helmet from her and help her out of my jacket. "I took every precaution. I would never let anything happen to her."

"It was so much fun, Dad." Amelia walks up the steps and kisses his cheek. "I want to do it again."

"No."

She rolls her eyes. "You worry too much."

"Amelia," Max says, softening his voice and putting his arm around her. "If anything were to happen to you."

She looks over her shoulder at me. "Viktor wouldn't let me get hurt."

"I know, sweetheart. I trust Viktor. It is everyone else I do not trust."

"What will you do in a few weeks when I'm in California?" She smiles.

"I'm working on that."

When Amelia first moved in with Max and Irina, she was timid, like a frightened kitten. She'd been through hell at the hands of Moreno and the other sick bastards in Mexico. Amelia was wary of most men, but she seemed most intimidated by Max. Most days, she spent glued to Irina's side.

Watching the two of them today is amusing. You'd never know there were ever any obstacles in their relationship. This little redhead isn't afraid to challenge her father. I don't know how he'll manage when she's halfway across the world.

"You only have two weeks left," she says in a sing-song voice as she walks into the house.

"Don't remind me," Max says too quietly for her to hear. Then, he looks at me. "We need to talk."

"Now?"

"Meet me in my office in fifteen minutes."

Maxim

I WALK BACK INTO THE HOUSE AND HEAD TO MY OFFICE. That child is going to be the death of me. If I thought Svetlana gave me a hard time, Amelia has her beat. At least Lana was interested in the lifestyle, and I was able to set up some protection for her.

But Amelia is very different. She's aware of the lifestyle Irina and I share. At first, she was confused and frightened. Amelia asked Irina to be included in one of her sessions because she feared Irina was being abused by me. Although her parents had a healthy relationship, once they passed away, all she experienced was dysfunctional foster homes and then the depravity of Moreno's men.

Irina attended several sessions alone with Amelia before I was asked to join. It was difficult for me to hear Amelia's fears, but given her experiences, I understood their root cause. With words, I reassured her of my love for Irina and her and Lana.

But it took time for her to observe that my words matched my actions. That no matter what, I would protect the three of them —even if that meant giving my life in exchange for theirs. Little by little, Amelia warmed up to me. Eventually, she allowed me the privilege of earning her trust. Today, no one would ever question my spunky red-headed daughter, and I ever struggled with our relationship.

Now, it is my turn to struggle. Amelia trusts me, and she tolerates my men. I trust every one of them with her life. However, I will not force her to be uncomfortable as she embarks on this new chapter in her life.

At the same time, I cannot allow her to go to California without security. I have too many enemies who would love to get at me through someone I love, and Viktor just added to the list with the Albanians. We have come to an agreement, but I do not trust them. Trust is something to be earned, and it does not come easy in this business.

There is a knock on my office door. Igor pops his head in. "Viktor's here."

"Send him in."

The door opens wider, allowing Viktor to enter my office.

"Have a seat."

He sits across from me, a wary look on his face.

"How are you feeling?" I ask.

"I'm doing better." He lifts his hand and moves his fingers. "There's still some occasional numbness, but Kasimir says that should eventually go away."

Viktor is a lucky man. The bullet missed his major organs by a fraction of an inch. If Dimitri had not attempted to stitch up the wound, he most likely would not have made it.

"I know you have been anxious to get back to work, but the situation with the Albanians has complicated things."

"I screwed up. I'm sorry. I—"

I hold up my hand, stopping him. "We have already taken care of that. I have found a job that will keep you off the Albanian's radar while allowing you to get back to work."

"Oh?" He tilts his head. "What is it?"

"You will be accompanying Amelia to California as her personal security?"

"I'll be what?"

"No other members of my team are suitable for this job because of her comfort level. You are the only one Amelia feels safe with."

"Why me?"

"Because Natalie trusts you, and Amelia trusts Natalie."

"Oh." Darkness shadows his face. "When are we leaving?"

"Two weeks."

Viktor

I leave Maxim's office, my whole word feeling off-kilter. I've been waiting for a new assignment, but being put on security detail for Amelia was not on my radar. My phone just alerted me that the email from Max with all the info about the city, school, and house he's already purchased has arrived.

I head out back to the patio so I can sit and look through everything he sent me while I try to wrap my head around my new assignment.

Amelia wanted to live in the dorm, but Max wouldn't hear of it because she couldn't have security there. So, instead, he bought a four-million-dollar beachfront property. I click on the link he sent me and pull up an extraordinary home that is right on the shores of Long Beach, California.

Facing the water are two-story arched windows ensuring a panoramic view from anywhere inside the house. Max assured me the windows have already been replaced with bulletproof glass—he leaves nothing to chance. The interior is a modern three-bedroom, three-bath home complete with a kitchen that would be any chef's dream. "You never do anything small, do you?" I say and laugh.

"I guess he told you," Amelia says as she walks over to me.

"He did."

"Can you even believe him?" She blows out a frustrated breath as she sits in the chair next to me. "I wanted to live on campus and be like any other incoming freshman, but no. Dad has to go and buy me an outrageously expensive beach house. I'm not trying to sound ungrateful. I just wanted to feel normal for once."

I'm caught in that proverbial spot—between a rock and a hard place. I understand Amelia's desire to be like every other student. No matter how much she wants that, she's Maxim Solonik's daughter, and that association comes with strings attached.

"Try to see it from his point of view," I say, putting my phone on the small table next to me. "Maxim and Irina lost their daughter. Even with all of his connections, he was still helpless to save her. And all that happened right here. You want to go to the other side of the world—alone."

"But I'd be on campus with everyone else."

"I know, but that doesn't guarantee your safety," I explain. "Your last name now ties you to Maxim and everything, good and bad, that comes with what he does. He sees that he almost lost you before he got the chance to even know you existed. He's not going to let anything go to chance now."

Amelia sighs.

"It won't be as bad as you think. I'll keep my distance so you can have your space."

She looks at me with expressive brown eyes, "I'm glad Dad chose you."

I'm not sure how to respond. I wanted to return to work, but I wasn't anticipating this kind of assignment. "Yeah. Me too."

Amelia

"Viktor's less than thrilled about going to California with me," I say to Natalie on our video call.

"He'll come around," she reassures me.

I hope she's right. Otherwise, it's going to be a long, uncomfortable four years.

"Are you all packed?"

"Yep." I look over at my suitcases, and my eyes fill with tears.

"What's wrong, honey?" Natalie asks.

"I don't know. I'm happy, sad, nervous—everything all at once." I swipe at the tears that are now wetting my face. "I want to go, but at the same time, I don't want to leave."

"I completely understand. I felt that way when I first left for school, too. But, once you get there and make friends, you'll have a great time."

"I hope you're right."

"I am. You'll see." She smiles. Rose starts crying in the background. "She's ready for her nap. I have to go, but call me when you get there and get settled."

"I will. Love you, Nat."

"Love you too, Amelia."

I didn't get any sleep last night. Instead, I tossed and turned both from anxiety and excitement. As the hours tick by slowly, I take the time to look back over the past few years of my life.

I'll never forget that day in school. I was summoned to the principal's office. He was sitting there with an older woman whose hair was pulled back in a tight bun, a stern look on her face.

"Amelia Parker?" she asked.

"Yes."

"Amelia, come sit down," Mr. Walker said.

"Ms. Parker, your parents were killed in a car accident earlier today," the woman said. "I understand you have no other family."

She looked at me expectantly, as if I was supposed to be able to answer her question after she'd spit out words that changed my entire life. I didn't speak that day or for several weeks to come.

I left the school with Miss. Imogene and was put in my first foster home. It was also my last foster home.

The first two weeks were okay. The Harrisons were an affluent family. They had one child, a son, Seth. He was eighteen. They were so happy to have a daughter. I had my own bedroom with a beautiful canopy bed. Mrs. Harrison brought me shopping and filled my closet with more clothes than I'd ever seen. They enrolled me in a prep school and saw to it that I was able to continue my piano lessons. They would never replace my parents, but I started feeling safe and talking again.

Then, one night after I was asleep, Seth came into my room—into my bed. He put his hand over my mouth to keep me from calling out, and then he put his hand down my pajama shorts. I tried to fight him. I scratched and clawed at him, but he held me down. He told me if I ever said a word, he'd tell everyone it was me who sneaked into his room. Me who came on to him.

So, one night, when Seth was out with his friends, I climbed out my bedroom window and started running. I never looked back.

Living on the streets was preferable to spending another night in the Harrison's home, or so I thought. Three nights later, I was tucked away between two buildings. I was so tired. I'd only closed my eyes for a few minutes when I felt strong arms wrap around me.

"Don't make a sound," he said. *"Or you'll regret it. Do you understand?"*

I nodded.

"You're going to walk with me like a good little girl, and we're going to get into my car."

He squeezed my arm and dragged me alongside him. Then, he opened the backdoor and shoved me in. There was another man in the backseat. He held up a syringe. I tried to move. Tried to get away, but it was no use. I felt a prick and then nothing.

The next time I opened my eyes, I was in hell.

I was at Moreno's for six months when Natalie got there. She kept promising that her boyfriend would get us out of there, but I didn't believe her. Nor did I ever think I'd have a family—a place where I belong.

But I do have it. I have a mom and dad and a big sister. The past two years of my life have been more than I ever thought possible. And today, I'm willingly walking away from it.

My door cracks open. "May I come in?" Lana asks.

"Sure." I sit up in bed.

"I had a suspicion you'd be awake."

I yawn. "I didn't sleep much last night."

She sits on the bed next to me. "I remember the night before I left for New York City. I didn't sleep a wink. I was scared to leave behind the only life I knew, but at the same time, I was excited to see what the future held for me."

"That's exactly how I feel."

"It's going to be a big adjustment. There were days I wanted to call Papa to bring me home."

"Why didn't you?"

"Alex." Lana smiles. "He forced me to go out, meet people, and explore the city."

"I don't have an 'Alex.'" My heart sinks. I don't want to end up calling Dad to come back home.

"You'll have Viktor. He'll make sure you're okay." Lana gives me a hug. "I'm going to miss my little sister, though."

"California's only a plane ride away." I smile.

Amelia

I'VE NEVER CARED ABOUT THE MONEY MY PARENTS have. In the whole scheme of life, it's irrelevant. But right now, I'm thankful for it. Saying goodbye is proving harder than I thought. I haven't been able to stop crying—which is why I'm grateful we're in a private hangar.

"I'm counting on you to take care of my little girl," Dad says to Viktor.

"You know I will."

Viktor's a tough read. He's large and imposing. That alone is enough to scare most people. But underneath his tough exterior, I know there's a tender man. I've seen the way he was with Natalie and Rose. He used to look so happy until Alex came back. Now he's so closed off. He doesn't talk much, and he rarely ever smiles. But I know he's safe. That's what I'm hanging onto. Otherwise, the knowledge that he's going to be my roommate, the only person I'll know, is unsettling.

"Oh honey," Mom comes over and wraps me in her arms. "I'm going to miss you so much."

"Me too, mom." I sniffle and swipe at the tears pouring down my face.

"Are you sure this is what you want to do?"

"I'm sure." I try to sound as brave as possible.

"We're only a phone call away," she says and hugs me tight.

Dad pulls Viktor off to the side. It looks like they're discussing something important, but they're too far away to hear what's being said. Their conversation ends with a handshake, and then Viktor walks up the steps into the jet. Dad remains off to the side. Mom and Lana are busy talking with the pilot, so I make my way over to him.

"Everything okay?" I ask as I sidle up to him.

Dad puts his arm around me. "Yes. Everything is okay."

Guilt washes over me. "Would you rather I stayed here? I can find a school—"

"My sweet daughter, I am excited for you but sad for me. I feel like we have just found you, and you are ready to spread your wings and fly so quickly." He places a kiss on top of my head. "I will never allow my reservations to hold you back. I want you to chase your dreams."

"When I was in Mexico, I knew my days were numbered. But you gave me a second chance," I say quietly. "Thank you for everything you've given me. I promise to make you proud of me."

"Amelia Solonik, I am already proud of you."

My tears start falling again as I wrap my arms around my father's neck. "I love you."

"*Ya lyublyu tebya malen'kaya ptichka.*"

Before I lose my nerve, I run up the steps to the plane.

It's only a few minutes until the door is closed and the plane's engine roars to life. I wave goodbye through the plane's tiny windows, and then we're taking off to start my new adventure.

Viktor

Amelia's sobbing as the plane's wheels lift from the ground, and we take flight.

"You okay, kid?"

"Mhm." She nods.

I'm lacking in the feelings department. With Natalie, everything came so naturally, but I don't know what to say to this girl. She cries until she's fast asleep. I unbuckle and grab a light blanket from the bedroom. Carefully, I lay her seat back, and she stirs. Her eyes flutter open.

"It's okay. It's just me. I have a blanket for you," I say quietly and put the blanket over her.

"Thank you," she whispers, then cuddles up with the blanket and falls back asleep.

I pop in my earbuds and settle in for the long flight.

The flight attendant comes into the room to let me know we're approaching JFK. We have to land to refuel. I'm hit with an

150

onslaught of feelings when I look out the window and see the New York City skyline lighting up the night. There are so many memories of Natalie attached to this place—this city.

"Amelia." I gently shake her shoulder. "You need to put your safety belt back on. We're getting ready to land."

Amelia rubs her eyes. "Already?"

"Already? It's been eleven hours."

She shoots up in her seat. "Are you serious?" She leans over me to look out the window. "I've never landed here at night. Look at all those lights. It's incredible."

"It is. Now sit down and buckle up, please."

Amelia slides back into her seat and buckles her lap belt. "How long are we going to be here?"

"Just long enough to refuel."

"Oh."

"Why?"

"I was hoping maybe I could see Natalie while we're here."

My heart stops beating. "We won't make it there and back in time. But you can call her while we're on the ground."

"Okay." Her shoulders slump.

The wheels of the plane touch down, and we taxi to a stop.

"I'm getting off with the pilot. I need you to stay on here with the flight attendant, okay?" I don't want to be around while she's talking to Natalie.

"That's fine."

"Are you hungry?"

"Yes, very."

"Do you want me to have the flight attendant make us something from the plane, or would you prefer some fancy airport food?

"A greasy burger sounds delicious."

"I'll see what I can find for us. You better be right here when I get back," I warn.

<h1 style="text-align:center">Amelia</h1>

AMELIA

Open mouth, insert foot, Amelia. Why did I ask Viktor if we could visit Natalie? That was the world's dumbest question. Of course, he's not going to want to see her. It's only nine o'clock. She should still be awake. I pull out my phone to call her while Viktor's gone. I tap her contact and wait for her to pick up.

"Hello?" Natalie's voice comes through a second before the video connects.

"Hi. I hope it wasn't too late to call."

"Not at all. Where are you?"

"In New York. We had to land to refuel."

"I wish things were different. I'd love to see you before you leave."

"Me too."

We talk for a bit longer. Rose makes a brief appearance with Alex before he puts her to bed. She's getting so big. I didn't realize kids grew so quickly. I tell her all about the house Dad bought and how nervous I am to start school.

"I think I better go. Viktor's on his way back."

152

"Okay, honey. Have a safe rest of your trip, and we'll talk soon."

We hang up right as Viktor enters the plane. He holds up a bag of food.

"I come bearing gifts." He grins.

"That smells like a burger and fries."

"It is."

My stomach growls, and I laugh.

"Sounds like I'm just in time."

Viktor pulls out the food, and we start eating. We've never really spent a lot of time alone together, so there are long, awkward pauses in our conversation. If this is how things are going to be between us, our living situation isn't going to work.

"You look deep in thought," Viktor says.

"I am." I struggle to look into his eyes.

It's something that was forbidden when Moreno had me. My therapist at Jelena's Hope worked on it with me for a very long time. It still doesn't come naturally, but I can do it most of the time.

When I do meet his gaze, my breath catches. His eyes are the most beautiful shade of sapphire blue. I've never seen eyes like his. It's easy to get lost in their depths and the stories they look like they hold.

"Everything okay?" he asks.

"Oh, yeah, sorry," I stumble over my words. "I was just thinking we're about to be roommates, and we really don't know one another."

"I'm sure it'll be fine. You'll be busy with school and your friends."

"I'm not big on social things. I'll most likely be spending a lot of time at home. So, we need to get to know one another."

"How do you suggest we do that?" he asks.

"We can ask each other questions." As soon as the words leave my mouth, I realize how juvenile they sound. "Never mind, pretend you never heard that."

Viktor chuckles. "How about we just let it happen naturally?"

"That sounds like a better idea." I smile.

"Excuse me," the flight attendant says. "We're about to take off again."

"Thanks." Viktor nods, and she goes back into the staff area. "Are you ready to become a California girl?"

Viktor

IT'S CLOSE TO FOUR A.M. WHEN WE STEP OFF THE JET AT LAX and make our way into a private hangar where the dark grey Audi e-Tron Quattro Max purchased for us is waiting.

"Wow." Amelia runs her hand across the hood. "Dad never does anything halfway, does he?"

"Never." I laugh.

An employee unloads our luggage from the plane, and I get it all into the car. It's a tight fit. The car is gorgeous but not made for transporting a lot of stuff.

"Ready?" I ask Amelia.

"I think so."

I open her door, and she slides her petite frame into the car. Then I round the car and get behind the wheel.

Thankfully, the traffic isn't as heavy as I'm told it can get on the highways here, and we make it to our new house in a little over an hour. I turn onto our palm tree-lined driveway and pull the car into the garage under the house.

"Viktor?"

"What's up?"

"Before we go in, can we go to the beach and watch the sunrise?"

The night sky is already giving way to the twilight of the early morning.

"I think we can manage that."

She rewards me with a smile. We walk out the door that leads us outside and to the entrance of our private beach. Amelia freezes when the ocean comes into view. I stand next to her.

"I've never been to the beach," she says quietly without taking her eyes off the water.

"For real?"

She nods her head.

"Come on." I take her by the hand. "Let's go down to the water."

Amelia follows me onto the sandy beach. I stop, take off my shoes, and roll my pants up.

"Take your shoes off."

"Why?"

"So we can get in the water."

"I don't know about that," she says, eyes wide.

"Why not?"

"There's so much of it, and the waves are so big."

The waves today are actually relatively tame. Wait until she sees the sea during a storm.

"Do you trust me?"

"Yes," she says hesitantly.

"Take off your shoes. I won't let anything happen to you."

She slips off her sandals and follows me to the water's edge. The water is warm as the waves lap at our feet. We stand there for a few minutes and watch as the sun peeks over the horizon. The sky becomes a canvas of pinks and purples as a new day is born.

I take a few more steps into the water. "Come on over."

"I'm scared."

"I'll hold onto you." I reach my hands out.

It takes a minute, but she finally places her hands in mine and takes tentative steps closer. I take a few more steps backward, the water nearing my knees. My pants are soaked, but I don't care. It's fitting that the first thing Amelia experiences is the ocean.

My back is to the oncoming waves, so I'm not prepared when a bigger wave crashes around us. Amelia loses her footing. I grab her by the waist, but it's too late. She's soaked from head to toe. I freeze, not knowing how she's going to react.

When she stands back up, Amelia laughs. A sweet, pure laugh. I can't help but join her.

"I must look like a drowned rat."

"You look fine." I tuck a curly red lock of hair behind her ear. "Do you want to go closer to the shore?"

"No. This is fun."

I keep her close to me while we let the waves splash around us and the sun lights up the sky. Once the vibrant colors give way to bright blue, we make our way out of the water. Amelia grabs her shoes and her cell. "Selfie?" she asks.

"It's the least I can do for getting you all wet."

She holds the phone out for our picture, but she's too short to get the both of us in the shot.

"May I?"

She passes me the phone, and I snap a few pictures.

"Thank you."

"It was my pleasure." We begin walking back to the house. "Why don't you go inside and get dried off? I'll get our stuff."

Amelia

The ocean is enormous. I felt so small and insignificant standing at the water's edge. Then, Viktor wanted me to follow him in. I was so scared. But when he put his hands out and asked me to trust him, something drew me to him. There was no way I could resist.

I flip through the pictures he took of us. We're both sopping wet. I'm grinning from ear to ear while Viktor barely cracks a smile. I'll have to get these printed and framed—our first moments in California.

Carefully, I make my way through the house, trying not to get everything wet and sandy. I go into the first bedroom I find and head straight into the bathroom to take a shower.

After I'm sure I got all the sand out of my hair, I turn off the water and grab a fluffy blue towel. Mom and Dad made sure the house was not only fully furnished but had everything in it so we'd feel at home when we got here.

I peek out of the bathroom and find my suitcases on the bed. I'm happy because I didn't consider needing clean, dry clothes after my shower. After I dress and comb my hair, I go back into the main room. I don't see Viktor anywhere, but this house is pretty big. So, I decide to go exploring.

There's a massive kitchen with granite countertops and stainless-steel appliances. "I sure hope Viktor knows how to cook," I say, knowing cooking is not my strong suit. The kitchen opens to an expansive living room with a fireplace. But the part I'm drawn to is the windows. They open fully, joining the house to a balcony overlooking the ocean. I slide them open, and it's as though there are no barriers between inside and outside.

Then, I decide to check out all the other rooms. I find a half bath in the hallway. The next door is another bedroom. I come to one final door and open it. Viktor's standing in the room wearing only a towel.

"Oh my gosh, I'm so sorry," I say, turning away as quickly as possible.

"It's okay. I should've locked the door."

"I didn't hear you in here. I should've knocked."

"It's okay, Amelia."

I close the door and hurry back to my room, completely humiliated. I flop on the bed and grab my cell to call home.

"I've been waiting for you to call," Mom says.

"Sorry. We went down to the beach to watch the sunrise before we came inside."

"What did you think?"

"Oh, Mom. It was incredible. Let me text you the pictures." I take a second to attach the pictures to a text and hit send. "You should get them in a second."

"Look at the two of you. You're soaked." Mom laughs.

"I've never been to the ocean. Viktor brought me into the water. And, well, a wave got us."

"You never told us you never saw the ocean. We would've brought you."

"That's okay. I was there today, and it was amazing."

Mom and I talk for a while longer.

I have one week before classes officially start. Freshman orientation is in two days, so I'll get to see the campus in person since we only did a virtual tour. Then, I need to pick up my books.

"You have the credit card. Use it for whatever you want."

"Thank you. I'll pay you back as soon as I find a job."

"You'll do no such thing," Mom says. "And you don't need to worry about working while you're in school."

Max and Irina have been more than generous with me since I met them. I know they have more than enough, but I don't want to keep taking from them.

"I know that, but—"

"No buts. This is your time to experience everything you can. You'll go to work soon enough."

"Yes, ma'am."

"I love you and miss you already."

"Me too."

"Dad and I will come to visit you soon."

"Okay." I yawn. "I think I'm going to take a nap. My body doesn't know what time zone it's in."

"Talk to you soon, *moya malen'kaya ptichka*."

Amelia

"ARE YOU READY?" VIKTOR CALLS ME FOR THE THIRD time. "If we don't leave now, we're not going to get there on time."

But I still don't answer. I can't answer. I'm sitting on the floor of my bathroom, knees drawn to my chest. I'm nauseous. My heart is pounding, and I'm unable to move.

Viktor knocks on my door. "I'm coming in." I hear the bedroom door open. "Amelia?"

"I'm in here," I say quietly.

Viktor stands in the doorway. "What's wrong?"

"I can't go." Tears begin pouring down my face.

He sits next to me. "What's going on?"I drop my head onto my knees.

"Hey," he says softly.

Slowly, I lift my head, and he wipes the tears from my face. "What's wrong?"

"I'm having—" I struggle to take a breath. "A panic attack."

"Look at me. Let's slow that breathing down."

He inhales slowly, and I try to follow him, but my breath catches on a sob.

"That's okay, you're going to be okay. Just keep watching me."

I follow his slow inhales and exhales as he helps me through the worst of it. It takes a few more breaths until the fear starts to subside.

"Talk to me," he says. "What has you so scared?"

"I don't like the unexpected. I don't know what's going to happen today when we get there." I let out a breath of air. "I can't go."

"It's orientation, right?"

I nod.

"I'm guessing they'll take you on a campus tour. Show you where everything is. See if you have questions."

"What if there's a lot of people?"

"There might be. But I'll be with you."

"You'll stay with me?"

"It's kinda my job." The corner of his mouth lifts to a half smile.

I put my head back on the wall. "Maybe this was all a mistake? Maybe I should go back home?"

"You aren't going back home until you at least give this school a try. If you go and hate it, we'll talk about returning to Russia." He stands up, then takes me by hand, pulling me up. Then, he turns me to face the mirror. "Do you see that young woman?"

I nod.

"You are Amelia Solonik. You are brave and strong. You are going to crush this today. And I'll be by your side for every second of it."

I spin around and wrap my arms around him. It takes a second, but then I feel his muscular arms around my body. "Thank you, Viktor."

"No problem, kid." He lets go. "Take a second and get yourself put back together, and then we're out of here."

"Okay."

He leaves me alone in the bathroom. I rinse my face off and

touch up the small amount of makeup I was wearing. Then, with a final look at myself, I leave the safety of my bedroom and meet Viktor, who's waiting in the kitchen.

Viktor takes advantage of the 'sport' in the sports car and drives far too fast, but we make it just in time. A large group of students and parents are gathered outside the campus's main building.

It looks like Viktor and I are the last to arrive, and all heads turn our way as we approach.

"Can we go home?"

"No. You've got this."

A girl with long brown hair wearing a shirt with the school's shark logo on it approaches us. "Are you Amelia?"

"Yes. I'm sorry we're late."

"It's okay. We're just about to get started with the tour." She looks up at Viktor. "Is this your father?" she asks, uncertain.

"No." I giggle. "This is Viktor, my—" How do I tell them he's my bodyguard?

"I get it. Your boyfriend," she whispers conspiratorially.

"He's not—"

"It's all good. We can call him your rich uncle." She smiles and heads back to the front of the group, leaving me shaking my head.

"Hi, everyone. My name's Kinsley. I'll be your student representative." She turns to face the rest of the group. "Let's get our tour started. Follow me." She walks to the front and leads everyone into the Student Center Building.

"Do I have to start calling you Uncle Viktor now?" I whisper.

"Would you have rathered tell them I'm your father?" He tilts his head.

"Point well taken."

We stay toward the back of the group as Kinsley leads us

around the campus. Most of my classes are in the designated music buildings, so I shouldn't have difficulty navigating around. The tour concludes back where we started, and once Kinsley's answered everyone's questions, the group disperses.

"Do you mind taking a walk to the bookstore so I can pick up my textbooks?"

"Sure."

"So, when I'm at class, where will you be?"

"I'll be in the building close to your classrooms. Everything's been prearranged with the Dean."

"Oh." Part of me is relieved knowing Viktor will be nearby. The other part of me feels like I'm going to stick out from the crowd. "What am I supposed to tell people, for real, when they ask who you are?"

"It's up to you. You can tell them the truth or that I'm a friend. Whichever is easier for you."

"Don't you think they'll wonder why my *friend* follows me around campus every day?"

"Just tell them I go here too."

Seeing how every girl we passed couldn't stop staring at him, I'm sure whatever story I go with will cause drama. They'll be catty and jealous, or they'll be after me to set them up with him. Either way, it doesn't much matter. Making friends doesn't come easy for me.

Friends tend to ask about your family and your past. There's not much I can say about my adoptive family, and my past is something I'd rather not talk about—it's too painful. But really, who'd want to be friends with a girl that's been trafficked and raped? No one. So, it's easier to go to school, keep my head down, do my work, and come home.

Looking at it now, I guess Dad knew better than me about not living on campus. I thought it was something I'd try, but being here today, surrounded by people, reminds me why I need that quiet space. Next time I call, I'll have to apologize for giving him a hard time.

Amelia

TODAY'S THE FIRST DAY OF CLASS. TO SAY I'M NERVOUS is an understatement. I spent last night trying on every piece of clothing I brought with me, plus the ones I bought here. Viktor was a good sport. He stayed patient as I showed him each one, hoping to get his opinion on what I should wear. In the end, he wasn't much help. He told me everything looked pretty, which was sweet, but I still didn't have an outfit to wear. I ended up going to my room and video-calling Natalie and Lana to get their opinions. Finally, the three of us settled on a soft pink sundress and a pair of sandals.

I got up early to make sure I had enough time to do my hair and put on makeup.

"Amelia," Viktor calls from outside my room.

"Come on in." He opens the door but stays in the doorway. "I made breakfast. Come and eat."

The thought of trying to swallow food makes my stomach turn. "I'm not really hungry."

"Wrong answer." He smiles. "You need to have something in your stomach."

"Fine."

When I get to the kitchen, I see he's made one of my favorite breakfasts. When my parents were still alive, we had several avocado trees on our property. My mom used to make avocado toast for me. My favorite variation has tomatoes and balsamic vinegar, exactly like what's on the plate in front of me.

"How did you know?"

"I have my ways." He grins. "Now, sit and eat."

Viktor loads the dishwasher while I have breakfast. "Aren't you eating?"

"I had an omelet. I'm not much for avocado anything."

"But you've never tasted this."

"And I never will."

"Come on, just take one bite." I bring a piece of my toast over to him. "If you don't like it, you never have to eat it again."

He leans down and bites into the toast. I watch his face as he chews.

"Well?"

"It wasn't bad."

"Told you so." I smile and take the last bite.

I go to grab my plate and glass to load the dishwasher.

"I've got it. Go finish getting ready."

I touch up my lipstick, and then, with a final spin in front of the mirror, I'm ready to go. I grab my backpack and search for Viktor, who I find on the balcony, watching the waves roll in.

Setting my backpack on the couch, I join him on the balcony. For a few minutes, neither of us speaks. I'm enjoying the feel of the warm breeze and the cadence of the waves. It's almost hypnotic.

"Are you ready to go?" he asks.

"As much as I hate to leave this." I motion out toward the water. "I have to get to class."

I go to grab my backpack, but Viktor gets to it first.

"You don't have to carry it. I'm perfectly capable."

"You'll be lugging it around all day. The least I can do is bring it to the car for you."

"This car looks like so much fun to drive."

"It's not bad." Viktor smiles. "Do you want to drive when we get off the highway?"

"I'd love to. But I don't know how."

"You don't have your license?"

I shake my head. In Russia, Dad never let me out alone. Either he drove or one of the security team did. There was no need for me to have a license.

"Do you want to learn?"

"I'd love to, but I don't think Dad would approve."

"Let me handle him."

Amelia

Somehow, we still manage to get to campus early enough to park and take a leisurely stroll to the music building. Mondays are going to be busy days. First up is my History of Music class. After that, I have my private piano lesson, and then I have a U.S. History course. Viktor walks me to my classroom. That's where my brave façade cracks and I panic.

"I want to go home," I say quietly.

Viktor takes my hand and leads me to a quiet corner in the hall. "Keep your eyes on me and slow your breathing down. Today's going to be the hardest—the first day always is. But I'll be right out here." He points to a bench in the hallway near the classroom. "You have your phone. Text me if you need anything."

I nod, afraid if I speak, the tears I'm holding back will fall.

We breathe together for a few more minutes until I feel my heart rate slow and my muscles relax.

"Are you okay now?"

"I think so."

"You're going to do great."

"I'll see you after class." I manage a small yet uncertain smile and walk back toward the classroom.

A tall, bronze-skinned guy walks up to the door at the same time as me. He pulls it open. "After you," he says.

"Thank you," I answer shyly.

After a quick scan of the classroom, I decide on a desk in the back corner. The guy follows me and takes the desk next to me.

"I'm Mateo," he says.

"Amelia."

"You're not from around here, are you?"

"Nope. I'm from Russia."

He tilts his head. "A Russian with an Australian accent?"

"It's a long story."

"Gotcha." He smiles. "Do you live on campus?"

"No."

Thankfully, the professor calls the class to order, and our conversation is interrupted.

The first half of class is spent reviewing the syllabus's significant points. Then, the professor moves right into his lecture. I'm thankful when class is over because my hand is already tired from taking so many notes. I slide my notebook into my backpack and walk to the door.

"What instrument do you play?"

"Piano. What about you?"

"Guitar."

Once I get into the hallway, I look around for Viktor and find him leaning against the wall a few doors down. I can tell the second he notices Mateo's nearness to me. He pushes off the wall and walks toward me.

"It was nice meeting you, but I have to be going."

"Catch ya later," Mateo says with a smile. Then, he heads down the hall in the opposite direction.

"And you thought you wouldn't make any friends."

"I'd hardly call him a friend. He sat next to me, and we chatted a little."

"Looked to me like he was very taken with you."

"You're crazy. Did anyone ever tell you that?" I laugh.
"Many times."
"I have to get to my piano lesson. I'll see you later."

Viktor

She's only been to one class, and already, she has a guy interested in her. Part of me wanted to rush over and tell him to back off—like Maxim would've done. But I can't do that. I need to give her space while keeping a close eye. Amelia deserves to spread her wings. To build some confidence in herself.

I watch as she disappears into the music room. There's a bench across from the door that allows me to see inside the classroom. I grab a seat and pull out my phone to keep busy while she has her lesson. I'm told she's excellent, but I've never heard her play. Max ordered a piano for the house. It's scheduled for delivery next week.

Amelia warms up with some scales. Then she moves to a classical piece I recognize immediately. I set my phone down to listen to her play "Waltz No. 2" by Dimitri Shostakovich.

The song sparks a memory from when I was a boy. Papa converted part of our home into a studio so Mama could continue dancing. I close my eyes and see Mama in a flowy white ballet dress as she twirls on her toes. Waltz No. 2 plays on the record player in the corner of the room. She looks like an angel.

Of all the classical pieces, Amelia's playing one that holds such vivid memories for me.

After she goes through that classical piece several times, she switches to a modern song. I recognize it right away, "Scars to Your Beautiful" by Alessia Cara. Then, she begins singing. Her voice, the lyrics. It's as if the song was written for her. I walk over to the door to watch her closer. Her eyes are closed. She's fully immersed in the moment, and she's drawn me right into it with her.

Until the same boy from early comes up next to me and looks through the window.

"Wow," he says. "She's really good."

"Yes, she is." I return to my spot on the bench, and he sits beside me.

"Do you know her?"

"I do."

"Are you two *together*?" he asks cautiously.

"That's for her to tell you. If she chooses."

He nods and goes back to listening. After Amelia's lesson, she opens the door and steps into the hallway. Shock registers on her face when she sees the two of us sitting on the bench.

The boy pops up as soon as he sees her. "You sing and play perfectly."

"Thank you." Her cheeks turn pink. "What's going on here?"

"I don't know about him." The boy waves his thumb in my direction. "But I have a guitar lesson."

"Viktor, this is Mateo. Mateo, this is my friend, Viktor." Amelia introduces us.

"Good to meet you," Mateo says and reaches his hand out to me.

I stand but don't reciprocate the gesture. "Nice to meet you."

Mateo turns back to Amelia. "A few friends and I have a band. We're looking for a new keyboard player. Do you think you might be interested?"

Amelia glances over her shoulder at me. I shrug. This is up to her.

"I might be."

"What's your cell number? I'll text you the information." Amelia relays her number, and Mateo puts it into his contact. Her phone dings a second later. "Now you have my info, too."

"Thanks."

"I gotta run. I'll send everything after my lesson." With that, he disappears into the classroom.

"What do you make of that?" she asks. "I don't know that I'm good enough to play in a band."

"What are you talking about? You're amazing."

The sound of Mateo playing his guitar comes from the music room. Part of me hoped he was no good, so she wouldn't be interested in his band. But unfortunately for me, the kid is talented.

I won't mention this little development to Maxim until I'm sure it's a definite. Something tells me he'll lose it if he hears his daughter wants to play in a band.

Amelia

I'M FINISHING UP MY LAST CLASS OF THE DAY. SO FAR, the music classes seem pretty easy. That's only because of the music education Maxim allowed me to pursue. It's given me an advantage over many other students, but I'm sure we'll all end up on an even playing field shortly. The U.S. History course, though, will take some extra studying.

When I get out of class, I look for Viktor and find him waiting at the end of the hall. It looks like he's just ending a phone call. He slides his cell into his pocket, his back to me.

"Ready to go?" I come up behind him and poke him in the sides.

Viktor spins around like he's ready to attack. "Shit, Amelia. Don't do that."

His reaction startles me, and the smile falls from my face. "I'm sorry."

He softens his features. "It's okay. I'm just not used to that." He reaches out and slides my backpack down my arm. "I'll take this. Your shoulder must be sore from carrying it around all day."

"It is a bit heavy."

We get back into the car and head toward home. The traffic's quite a bit heavier than this morning. These commutes back and forth are going to get old really quickly. Viktor's patient and doesn't seem bothered by it. But I'm thankful that some of my classes are remote, so we don't have to do this every day.

"I got the information you'll need to get your driver's permit."

"You did?"

The school needs to verify my student status with the state. Once that's done, I can apply for my permit online.

"I made an appointment to take care of the paperwork Wednesday between your classes. I hope that's okay."

"That's perfect. Thank you so much." I can't help the smile that spreads across my face. "Wait until I tell my parents about the band and learning to drive."

"Can we hold off on that for a little while?"

I laugh. "Don't want Dad to freak out and show up here tomorrow?"

"Exactly."

"I can live with that."

Viktor takes an unfamiliar exit off the freeway.

"Is this a different way to get home?" Maybe he's trying to avoid some of the traffic.

"I planned a little surprise for us." He glances at me. "Is that okay?"

The familiar feelings of panic start to rise, but I take a few slow breaths to keep them at bay. "Surprises aren't my favorite. But I'm safe with you." I say those words out loud more for myself than for Viktor.

"I can tell you where we're going if it's easier."

"No," I say quickly. "I can do this."

"If it gets to be too much, just say the word. I want this to be fun, not scary."

I wring my fingers in my lap, trying to quell the nerves that are causing butterflies in my stomach. Before too long, we're pulling into a parking spot at a marina.

"Have you ever been on a boat?"

"Nope."

"Good." Viktor smiles. "It'll be another first."

We get out, and I follow him toward a large yacht where a man is waiting.

"Viktor?" the man asks when we get closer.

"Yes, sir." They shake hands. "And this is Amelia."

"It's a pleasure to meet you, Amelia. I'm Gus, and this is *Serendipity*." He motions to the yacht behind him.

"She's beautiful."

"Are you two ready to go?"

"We are." Viktor smiles proudly.

Gus steps into the boat, followed by Viktor, who turns and offers me his hand. Cautiously, I step from the dock into the boat. A few minutes later, we're moving slowly as the captain maneuvers us out of the marina and into the open water.

"Come with me," Viktor says, leading me to what he explains is the aft, where a table is set for two.

"What's this?"

"We're going to be having dinner in a bit. To celebrate the big move and your starting school."

My heart melts into a puddle. I've never had a man treat me so kindly. We stand by the rail and look out over the water.

"Look. There's a dolphin."

It turns out to be more than one dolphin. A large pod of dolphins is swimming and playing in the boat's wake. Several of them jump out of the water, making a big splash.

I reach into my pocket to grab my phone to take a video. "I left my phone in my backpack. In the car."

"I don't have mine either. We'll have to do this again to get pictures."

I'm disappointed that I won't have any videos or pictures from this trip. But that quickly dissipates, and we live in the moment instead. The dolphins continue their private water show for several minutes before they swim away.

"Have you ever seen dolphins before?"

"I haven't," he says.

"Good. It was a first for us both." My stomach tingles with excitement, knowing we shared a first.

We're both watching each other, saying nothing when a server opens a door, breaking whatever spell we were just under. He sets two glasses of sparkling water on the table.

"Dinner will be served in a few minutes," he informs us and disappears behind the same door.

"Shall we?" Viktor asks and pulls out a chair for me.

Dinner is served over several relaxed courses, starting with a Caesar salad and then a small cup of clam chowder. The main dish, lobster tails, is served just as the sun is beginning to set.

It looks as if the ocean is swallowing the sun. The sky has turned from a beautiful bright blue to a canvas of bright purples, pinks, yellows, and oranges. It's truly breathtaking. I don't want to take my eyes off it, but I also don't want this delicious food to go to waste.

The last course is a refreshing sorbet with a side of fresh fruit.

By the time we finish eating, the sky's dark and is filled with millions of twinkling stars. I go back to the rail and look up at the night sky. When I turn around, Viktor's watching me from the table.

"Thank you, Viktor. This was amazing." He's made me feel like the most special girl in the world. I know this wasn't a *real* date, but a girl can pretend, right?

"It was nothing."

"It wasn't nothing to me."

"Well, you're very welcome."

While the boat continues to sail, we sit in an oversized lounger. The air is getting chilly, and I shiver.

"Are you cold?"

"A little bit."

"I should've brought a sweater for you. Come sit close." He puts his arm around me to keep me warm.

I feel safe and protected.

And like I'm falling for a man I shouldn't be falling for.

178

Viktor

I fought Max on this assignment. Coming to California with Amelia wasn't on my radar as far as a job and was the last thing I wanted to do. But I'm glad he persisted. It's been good for me to keep busy—to think about someone other than myself.

Amelia's not your typical eighteen-year-old. She's a hard worker and takes her schoolwork very seriously. She spends hours each day practicing the piano, something that's quickly become one of my favorite times of the day. She's also a lot of fun to be around. Turns out we make pretty good roommates.

I never attended college. Didn't have a reason to. Once I graduated, I never wanted to sit in a classroom again. Sitting in the hallway isn't much better. It can get pretty boring, but it does give me the opportunity to find fun things for Amelia and me to do. Since we're both new here, I try to plan one night a week where we explore the area.

Of all her school days, my favorites are the days she has piano lessons. Today, she's working on a piece I don't recognize. I enjoy the quiet and listening to her play when Mateo appears and sits next to me.

"Hey, Viktor. What's up?"

"I'm listening to Amelia practice her recital piece."

"She's amazing, isn't she," he says with starry eyes.

I stare at him without answering until he takes his attention off Amelia and back to me.

"I'd like to ask Amelia on a date. My sister's getting married. It's going to be an upscale event at the country club my parents belong to," he says without taking a breath.

"Okay."

"Does that mean you'd have to tag along?"

"What do you mean?"

He looks to the door and back to me. "Amelia told me you're her bodyguard or something. Said her dad's really overprotective."

"You could say that."

"So, if I took her on a date, does that mean you'd have to come too?"

"Yes."

"I don't know how I'd explain to my parents that my girl-friend and her bodyguard are coming?"

What's this kid talking about? To my knowledge, and I make sure to be aware of everything, Amelia has not consented to be this boy's anything.

"Your girlfriend?" I ask and raise an eyebrow.

"Well, I'm hoping she will be."

"Let's see what she says before you start calling her your girlfriend."

"Okay." Mateo takes a deep breath. "That was awkward."

I force myself not to laugh. If he thinks that was bad, he hasn't seen anything yet.

The door opens, and Amelia walks out. She catches my eye, and a smile graces her face.

Mateo walks between us and over to her. "I wanted to talk to you."

"What's up?"

He looks back at me. "Can we go over there and talk alone?"

"We're good here," she says. She's still timid around other people, especially guys.

"Okay. Well, I wanted to ask if you'd be my date for my sister's wedding next weekend?"

"Oh." She looks surprised.

"It's going to be a fancy thing, so you'd get to dress up and all that girly stuff."

"I'm not sure," she says and looks at me. "Can I think about it and let you know?"

"Yeah, sure. It's no big deal if you can't make it." Mateo acts unphased by her lack of enthusiasm.

"I'll text you later." She walks over to me. "Ready to go?"

I feel bad for the kid. He's left standing there, defeated, as we walk away. He has no idea about the issues Amelia struggles with. She doesn't say much on our walk to the car. It isn't until we're halfway home that she finally speaks.

"That was unexpected."

"A bit."

"What do you think I should do?"

"That's up to you." I am not the one to be giving dating advice. "Maybe you should call Lana or Natalie?"

"Maybe." She turns and looks out the window. "Do you think he's safe?" she asks quietly.

She doesn't know I've done a little research on Mateo. His father, Everett Hart, is a big-shot attorney to the stars in Los Angeles. His mother, Willa Hart, is a stay-at-home wife and socialite. He has one sister, Summer Hart, an aspiring actress who is poised to marry Christopher Darby III, a partner in Mr. Hart's law firm. Their background checks have come back clean. Mateo doesn't pose any known threat to Amelia.

"I think he's as safe as any other twenty-year-old guy."

"How do you know how old he is?"

"It's my job."

"You did a background check on him?" she asks, shocked.

"Yes."

She puts her head back on the car seat. "Please tell me you didn't call Dad."

"I didn't call him yet."

"Please don't say anything to him until I decide what I'm going to do.

Amelia

When we get home, I head to my room to make a phone call. But not to who Viktor suggested. I love Lana, but we don't talk about guys. She doesn't know much about just regular dating, and I'm not interested in the lifestyle she lives. And I am not calling Mom. She'll give me great advice, but she doesn't keep anything from dad.

"Hi, sweetheart. You must be a mind reader." Natalie giggles.

"Oh?"

"I was going to call you this weekend. I have something to tell you."

"Really?" Sometimes, I worry I'm a bother to her, so hearing that she was going to call me makes me smile.

"Really. How's everything on the West Coast?"

"I guess it's okay."

"Just okay?" Natalie asks. "Is something wrong?"

"Not exactly. But don't worry about that. What did you want to tell me?"

"Nope, you first. What's going on?"

"Well, there's a guy, and I like him a lot."

"Oh my gosh, I'm so happy for you. Tell me all about him."

"He's gorgeous. Like not just good-looking, mouthwateringly gorgeous." We both laugh.

"Has Viktor checked him out?"

"He's been checked out. I'm safe with him." I mean, it's true.

"So far, so good."

"Most importantly, he's thoughtful and nice to me. He's always doing special things for me."

"That all sounds good."

"There's a problem, though."

"What is it?"

"I don't think he sees me as anything other than a friend." I sigh.

"I see," Natalie says. "The best relationships often start out as friendships."

"But how can I make it so we're more than just friends?"

"There's no real answer to that, sweetheart. The best thing you can do is continue to be friends. Keep getting to know one another, and don't try to force anything. If it's meant to be, it'll develop into more." She pauses. "You're in a new place with lots of different guys. If this guy is just a friend right now, don't be afraid to try going on some other dates. If he's really interested in you, he'll step up, and if not, maybe you meet the right one in the process."

"Yeah." That wasn't the advice I was hoping she'd give me.

"Just make sure Viktor checks everyone out first, please."

"I will. Now, what did you want to tell me?"

"I'm pregnant," Natalie squeals.

"Oh my gosh. Congratulations." My excitement threatens to bubble over. "Do you know if it's a boy or a girl? When are you due?"

"We just found out the other day. So far, only you and Lana know. And Alex, of course." Natalie says. "So, please don't tell anyone yet."

"I promise."

Finding out I'm going to be an aunt again distracts me from my problems.

"Is Rose excited?"

"We didn't tell her yet. I think she's a little too young to understand."

"She's going to be the perfect big sister."

Natalie and I talk about everything, baby. They're running out of room in their current apartment and are considering buying something roomier—whether or not to leave the city is a big consideration for them. When I look at the clock, I realize we've been on the phone for an hour.

"I should get going. I have a paper to write."

"It was wonderful to hear from you. Make sure you call me and keep me updated on this guy."

"I will. Can you not mention any of this to Lana and my parents? I'm not ready to tell them yet."

After we finish our goodbyes, I flop back on my bed. What answer do I give Mateo about the wedding? Viktor thoroughly checked him out, and he's safe, but Mateo isn't the one I want to be with. I think about what Natalie said. If I agree to go out with him, Viktor might get jealous and make a move. If not, at least I'll be having some fun with a nice guy.

Me: Is the offer still open to be your date for the wedding?

Mateo: It is, yes.

Me: I'd love to go

Mateo: Great. I'll pick you up at five on Friday. BTW- where do you live?

I don't know if I'm supposed to give that information out, so I go in search of Viktor. He's not in any of the main rooms, so I knock on his bedroom door.

"Come in."

I open the door and step into the doorway. "I told Mateo I'll go to the wedding with him next weekend. He wants to pick me up. Can I give him our address?"

"No. Find out where the wedding is, and I'll drive you."

"Can't we meet somewhere so he can take me himself?"

"No."

"You're as bad as my father, you know that?" I slam the door and go back to my room.

Me: I'm going to have to meet you there.

Mateo: Okay.

I can't believe I'm going on my very first date. I'm equally excited as I am nervous. My next problem is that I have nothing to wear. Viktor's going to have to take me shopping.

Viktor

AMELIA'S LAST CLASS OF THE DAY WILL BE OVER IN A few minutes. Then we're going shopping for a dress for the wedding. I've been holding off on telling Max about this Mateo kid. I was hoping he'd go away, but he isn't. I don't know what to do. Alex and I have been keeping in touch. He's pretty grounded and was Svetlana's keeper for a while. He'll know how to deal with this.

Me: I have a problem.

Alex: What's going on?

Me: Amelia has a date. I checked the guy out, and he's fine. But I haven't told Max. What do I do?

Alex: That is a dilemma. I'm going to suggest not telling him yet. You can let him in on it if it turns into more. There's no reason to alert him if it's just a one-time thing.

Me: Thanks. That helps.

Alex: There's something I need to talk to you about as well. Do you have a minute for a phone call?

Me: Sure.

What could be going on that Alex needs to talk to me? I walk to the end of the hall and find a quiet place. My phone vibrates.

"Hey."

"How's the West Coast treating you?"

"I got used to beach living very quickly." I chuckle. "How's Jelena's Hope NYC going?"

"Unfortunately, we keep busy. Somedays, it feels like a losing battle, but we'll keep up the fight as long as we need to."

"You're doing a good thing there, brother."

"Things aren't the same here without you."

"Yeah, well."

"There's something I need to tell you. I wanted you to hear it from me instead of someone else."

"Is everything ok?"

"It is." Alex pauses. "Natalie's pregnant."

I don't know what I expected Alex to say, but that wasn't it. I grab the wall for support while I let the news settle. This shouldn't surprise me. Natalie's a natural mom, and they're married. Of course, they'd want to extend their family. But in the world I used to live in, the one where Natalie and I were together, she'd be having my baby. This news puts things into a much different perspective. Natalie's moved on. I need to do the same.

"Congratulations. I'm happy for both of you."

"Thanks, Viktor. I really do appreciate it."

The classroom doors open, and students start filing out.

"I have to run. Amelia's getting out of class now."

"We'll talk soon."

I used the skills I learned in therapy. I felt the emotion and honored it for what it was. Now, I'm placing it in a neat box and putting it away. Life is moving on.

"Are you ready to go shopping?" Amelia's beaming.

"I can't wait." I laugh.

We find the boutique that was recommended to Amelia by another girl in her class. The sales lady, who introduced herself as Caroline, placed me in a cushiony chair outside the fitting rooms and instructed me to wait there. Then, she and Amelia disappear into the shop. When they return, Caroline has an armful of dresses.

"Time to try them on." She hasn't stopped smiling since we got here.

A few minutes later, Amelia comes out wearing a pink dress with puffy sleeves.

"What do you think?" she asks.

I glance up. "It looks fine."

She looks in the mirror, examining herself from all angles. "Nope. I don't like it."

She repeats the process with several more dresses. They all look the same to me, but she doesn't seem to like them.

"Last one," she says when she steps out of the changing area. "What do you think?"

I start to say it looks fine like all the dresses before, but when I look up, I'm speechless. Amelia's wearing a black off-the-shoulder dress that stops just above her knees. The dress hugs her curves. She looks grown-up and absolutely stunning, which is why she's not wearing this dress. "I don't like it. I think you should go with the first one."

"The pink one? Are you kidding?" She spins slowly in front of the mirror. "This is definitely the one."

I walk over and stand behind her, looking at her reflection in the mirror. "It makes you look far too grown-up. No."

She turns to face me, hands on her hips. Her ginger temper is about to make an appearance. "I'm not a child, Viktor. This dress fits perfectly." She runs her hands down her sides. "I'll be right back." She goes back into the changing area, where I'm hoping she removes the dress and puts something less—adult on.

When she comes back, she has her phone in her hand. She

snaps a few pictures in front of the mirrors and attaches them to a text.

"Who are you texting?"

"Natalie. Why?"

Good. Natalie's sensible. She'll tell Amelia this isn't the right dress.

It feels like hours before Amelia's phone dings. She reads the text and smiles before turning the screen to face me.

Natalie: That's the one. It looks hot. You're going to have that guy eating out of the palm of your hand. (you won't be "just friends" anymore)

Great. Natalie's encouraging her. I don't stand a chance with the two of them on the same side.

"See. She thinks it's perfect."

"Whatever." I return to my spot on the chair.

Amelia rolls her eyes and goes back into the dressing room. When she comes back out, she's in her clothes. Caroline's carrying the dress.

"I need to grab a pair of shoes, and then I'll be ready to go."

Amelia

I SKIPPED CLASSES TODAY TO GET MY HAIR AND NAILS done. Thankfully, Viktor didn't follow me into the salon. We need some space from each other. He's been in a mood all day. It's been nice to be alone and get pampered. My fingers and toes are painted a deep red, and the stylist is finishing my hair.

He hands me a mirror. "What do you think?"

Somehow, he worked magic with my unruly curls. The length of my hair is done in a French braid that's now elegantly pinned up in the back. Some of my corkscrew curls are hanging loosely, framing my face.

"It's beyond my expectations. Thank you so much."

"It was a pleasure, honey. I hope you have a terrific time on your date tonight."

After I finish paying, I leave the serenity of the salon and cross the sidewalk where Viktor's waiting by the car. I don't even bother to ask him what he thinks because I'll only get an unenthused *it's fine*.

Since there's already tension between us, I may as well tell him the rest of my news. It can't make things much worse.

"I told Mateo I'd join the band."

"What?" Viktor looks over at me. "You didn't even audition."

"He made a recording in the sound booth at school. The guys loved it."

"I see." Viktor narrows his eyes and grips the steering wheel tighter.

"I'll have rehearsal a few days a week, and they're booked every Friday and Saturday with different gigs."

"I need a list of all the venues."

"Why?"

"I have to check each one and make a decision on whether you can go."

"Wait a minute. You're here as security, not my father. I'm not asking for your permission."

"We're not having this argument while I'm driving."

"Fine." I turn to look out the window.

"Fine."

The rest of the drive is silent and tense. When he pulls into the garage, I don't wait for him to turn the car off before I grab my dress and get out. He follows on my heels.

"Amelia, wait."

"I can't. I have to get ready."

Viktor

I DON'T LIKE THIS TENSION AND FIGHTING BETWEEN Amelia and me. I wish she'd realize I'm only doing my job. It's my responsibility to keep her safe, but I can't do that if she doesn't tell me what's going on.

So, it's a good thing that when I sent Mateo a text, he readily gave me their list of venues. We agreed it was best not to tell Amelia. He's a good kid and wants to make sure she's not only safe but feels like a normal person.

"Viktor," Amelia says quietly. "Can you help me with the zipper?"

She's nervous. I can see it written all over her face. I need to get over myself and make sure she stays calm so she can enjoy her date. I make my way across the room to her. "Turn around." My hands shake as I slowly slide the delicate zipper up her back. "There, all done."

She turns around to face me. "Do I look okay?"

She's breathtaking. My body responds at the sight of her. "You look very pretty," I say and walk away quickly so she doesn't see my arousal.

I don't know why I'm reacting this way to her. All I know is my body better cut the shit. She's not only eighteen, but she's also my boss's daughter—she's totally off-limits.

"Viktor." She comes up behind me, placing her hand on my arm. "Can we please stop fighting? I don't like us being upset with each other."

"I agree." I turn around now that my dick is back under control. "Are you ready to go? I'm sure we'll hit traffic, and I don't want you to be late."

Mateo's waiting outside when we arrive at the country club. He's one of the groomsmen and is sporting a tux. The kid cleans up pretty well. I leave the keys in the car for the valet to park and make sure to get to Amelia's door before Mateo. Offering her my hand, I help her out.

"Thank you."

"Of course."

Mateo walks over. "Wow. You look hot."

I glare at him, but he doesn't seem to notice. He hasn't taken his eyes off Amelia.

"We need to go out to the garden. The ceremony will be starting in a few minutes."

He offers Amelia his arm and leads her to the wedding venue. I'm caught off guard by my feelings as I watch her walk away with him. You can't think those things, Viktor. She's not yours. She's allowed to date whomever she chooses. I silently repeat that, hoping it quells the jealousy that's stirring inside.

I leave a respectable distance, but I don't stray too far—Amelia is never out of my sight. It looks like she's having a great time. I don't think she's stopped smiling all evening. Finally, the DJ announces he's playing the last song. It's a slow dance. Mateo stepped away a few minutes ago, leaving Amelia at the table alone.

I'm just about to step in and ask her to dance when Mateo appears. He leads her to the dance floor. This time, he pulls her close to him. I see her tense up, but she doesn't pull away.

Then, he slides his hand down her back. She grabs his arm right before his hand lands on her ass. I can see her telling him something. Lucky for him, he readjusts his hold. My nerves are on a hairpin trigger. It wouldn't take much for me to rush in there and whisk her away if he doesn't respect her.

The song finishes, and the wedding guests slowly begin to disperse. I shoot Amelia a quick text telling her I'm going out to get the car and I'll meet her there. I give the valet our ticket and wait for him to pull the car around. It only takes a few minutes, and Amelia and Mateo still haven't come out. Do I go in and get her? And embarrass her? I can't do that to her, so I get in the car and wait.

Although I have my phone out, I'm not looking at the screen. Instead, I'm watching as Mateo and Amelia finally make their way outside. He leads her off the path to a dimly lit area. When I see him leaning in to kiss her, I set my phone aside, ready to intervene at any second.

Amelia

Mateo's family is lovely. They made me feel welcome, and I had a wonderful time. But now the wedding's come to an end. Viktor lets me know he'll be waiting in the car. Mateo takes me around so I can say goodbye and wish the new couple my congratulations before he walks me out the front doors. I think he's taking me to the car, but then he tugs my hand and leads me to a darker area off to the side.

My heart begins pounding as panic sets in. Why do I keep feeling this way? Mateo leans in, his lips pressing against mine. Breathing's getting harder. He pulls me closer and uses his tongue to part my lips. I can't take it anymore, and I put my hands on his chest to push him away.

"What's wrong?".

"I can't do this."

"It's just a kiss." He seems genuinely confused.

"Mateo, my history's complicated."

"Is that why you have a bodyguard? Has a guy hurt you?"

"Yeah." That's a mild way of putting it. "I need things to go slow. I get it if that's not what you want."

"I can go as slow as you need. The last thing I ever want to do is scare you."

I study his face to see if I can detect any crack in his demeanor. Any sign that he's lying, but I find nothing. Then, I glance over my shoulder at the car and find Viktor watching us intently.

My heart's torn. Mateo's a nice guy. He's closer to my age. But he doesn't make me feel like I do when I'm with Viktor.

"I really should get going."

"I'd like to take you out again," Mateo says.

I'm not sure how to answer him.

"You don't have to give me an answer right now."

"Can I think about it?"

We walk in silence until we get to the car. "You'll be at band practice tomorrow, right?"

"I wouldn't miss it for anything." Then I do something Viktor told me not to do. "I'll text you my address so you can pick me up."

Mateo's face lights up. "Will Viktor be okay with that?"

"Probably not, but I'll take care of it."

Mateo opens the car door for me. "Goodnight, Amelia." He kisses my cheek.

"Thank you for a wonderful evening." I slide into the car, and Mateo shuts the door.

He gives a small wave as we pull away.

Amelia

MATEO WILL BE HERE IN LESS THAN TWENTY MINUTES to pick me up for band practice. But I still haven't figured out how to tell Viktor. I'm pacing back and forth in my room, trying to find the words, when the doorbell rings.

"Oh no." He's early.

I rush out of my room, but Viktor's already answering the door.

"Hi. Is Amelia ready?"

"What are you doing here?"

"Amelia told me I could pick her up. We have band practice."

"She did, did she?" Viktor stands with his hand on the door, blocking Mateo from coming in.

"Hey Mateo," I chirp. "Come on in."

Viktor steps aside and gives me a look, letting me know we will be discussing this when we're alone. "You didn't tell me you were going out today."

"I was just about to." I shrug. "The band doesn't have a show tonight, so we're getting together for practice instead."

"And where is this practice happening?"

"It's at Quincy's house." Mateo jumps into the conversation. "Tristan's in the car waiting for us."

"You brought someone else here?" Viktor raises his voice.

"Um, yeah. Tristan doesn't have a car. I always pick him up on the way to practice."

"I'll be okay, Viktor. You can follow behind us," I say quietly.

There's fire in Viktor's eyes as he grabs the keys but doesn't say a word to me.

"We good?" Mateo asks.

"Sure." I smile nervously and grab his arm. "Let's go."

Viktor

THIS GIRL'S GOING TO BE THE DEATH OF ME. I specifically told her not to give out our address, but did she listen? Of course not. She did it anyway. Now, Mateo knows where we live, and so does his buddy. I don't think Amelia fully understands how many enemies Maxim has and the lengths they'll go to bring him to his knees.

And right now, tensions are high between Maxim and some of his new associates. Yes, I'm responsible for that, making giving our address even riskier. I don't trust the Albanians. Maxim made a deal with them, but that doesn't mean they've forgotten my transgressions. If they see an easy way to take me out, they'll take it.

I'm fuming as I follow Mateo's car to a house in what looks to be another affluent neighborhood a few towns over. He drives to the front of the house, and I pull in behind him.

"Is he coming too?" Tristan asks.

"They're a package deal," Mateo says.

"That must be fun when you two are—" The guy makes a lewd gesture, and I step forward, ready to punch him in the face. Talking about Amelia like that is unacceptable.

"Knock it off, Tris." Mateo elbows his friend.

Amelia looks uncomfortable but doesn't say anything.

"Come on, Viktor," Mateo says. "Practice is inside."

I follow the trio into the house. We walk down a long hall to another door and down a flight of steps.

"Quincy's parents converted this whole level into a studio for us."

That seems like a big commitment for a garage band.

"Amelia, this is Sparrow and Grayson." Mateo introduces her to the other members of the band.

"Nice to meet you both."

"You come highly recommended by Mateo here," Sparrow says.

"I hope I live up to whatever he's told you about me."

"So far, so good," Grayson adds.

Amelia tenses once again. I don't know if she's ready for this. She was doing great in Russia, but moving here brought back the panic attacks she used to suffer from. She has virtual sessions with her therapist at Jelena's Hope. It's helped. She's much more comfortable at school and at home. But being with four guys, three of whom are strangers, is a big stretch for her.

"Viktor, you can sit over there," Mateo points to a sitting area and then turns back to the group, "Let's warm up with "Two Steps Behind." You good with that one, Amelia?"

"Yep." She gets behind the keyboard, and I grab a seat off to the side.

I don't know what I expected, but this band is good. Like really good. And Amelia fits in as though she's played with them for years.

Gone is the tension from just moments before. Amelia's in her element. She looks genuinely carefree. I have my weekly call with Maxim tomorrow. It'll be a relief for him when I tell him she's found a good group of friends and is doing well.

Amelia

I'M FINDING IT ODD THAT THE SMALL GROUP OF friends I've amassed is a group of guys. At that first practice, I was a little unsure. Some of them were acting like jerks. But they've grown on me. I've even surprised myself with how comfortable I feel with them now. It feels like I have four older brothers looking out for me.

Mateo and I have been hanging out more. This is all new to me. I don't have the same feelings for Mateo that he does for me. But I decided it couldn't hurt to try Natalie's advice. So, I agreed to try out this dating thing as long as Mateo promised to go at my pace. Most of the time, he does a great job with that.

He knows I don't like being around crowds of people. Even though he prefers to be out in public doing things, he never complains when all I'm able to do is hang out at the house or go down to the beach for a picnic. He tells me I make him happy and how much he cares about me.

I think the best thing about Mateo is he treats me like a normal person. Would that change if he knew my history? Doesn't matter. We're not at a place where I'm ready to share that part of me. Right now, I'm enjoying our friendship. The problem

is my eyes and heart are drawn to the man who's always present in
the background.

Amelia

I'VE BEEN PLAYING THE PIANO FOR AS LONG AS I CAN remember. My earliest memories are of sitting on my dad's lap. I must've been only three or four. He'd take my tiny hands with his and teach me what each key was and how to make a song. He was an accomplished pianist and my very first teacher.

I knew my future would involve playing. I don't feel like a whole person without it. But I always pictured myself playing in an orchestra or something fancy. Being part of a rock band was never on my radar, but it's so much fun.

Death Rat, the crazy name for our band the guys picked, already has a great reputation and is in high demand at local venues. The guys are trying hard to get the attention of some A&Rs, who they tell me are basically talent agents that frequent some of the clubs and other places we play. If the right person discovers us, it could mean big things.

I haven't told my parents about it yet. I don't think they'll take the news that their daughter, who is supposed to be studying classical piano, is playing in a band called Death Rat. I can picture the look on Dad's face, and I laugh. I'll tell them eventually, especially if something big happens for us. But until that happens, I don't see any reason to upset my parents. I'm keeping this to myself and enjoying the ride.

Tonight's show was the biggest one we've played to date. Our audience was on fire, which really helped motivate us on stage.

My adrenaline's still running high when the show ends. The club planned a big afterparty for the band and our fans. They sold VIP admission tickets, and people are already gathering for it.

"You're going to stay for the party, right?" Mateo asks.

"I don't know. There's a lot of people."

"And they'll all want to see my girl to get her autograph and selfies. Please. I won't leave your side."

It's his eyes that get me every time. Sometimes, I watch him when he doesn't realize I'm looking. The grey turns dark and stormy. He doesn't show it on the outside, but I can almost feel the anger swirling inside him. Other times, they're a soft shade of grey that holds an immense sadness. But right now, they're sparkling with excitement, something I rarely see from Mateo.

"I'll stay for a little bit."

He gives me a huge grin and grabs my hand. "Come on. I can't wait to show my girlfriend off."

"Mateo, please don't introduce me as your girlfriend." Although I say the words, the music in the club is so loud he doesn't hear me.

On the way to the dance floor, we stop by a few people who want selfies and autographs. I think he introduces me to a few others. I smile since I can't hear what he's saying.

Finally, we make it to the dance floor. I try my best to relax and focus on Mateo, but there are too many people. They're dancing and brushing up against me. The loud music, the bass, and being touched toss me back in time—back to Mexico.

"I can't stay here," I say, not waiting for Mateo's response.

I rush off the dance floor and look around for Viktor. He's already coming to me.

"What's wrong?" He grabs my arms.

"There are too many people. I want to go home."

"Okay. Let's go." Viktor leads me to the door.

Mateo catches up and grabs my arm, making me flinch. "Where are you going?"

"Home."

"Why? Aren't you having fun?" Sadness has crept back into his eyes. "I wish you'd stay with me."

"I'm sorry, Mateo."

"I'll call you tomorrow." I grab Viktor's hand. "Can we go now?"

He nods, and although I was hoping he'd offer to leave with me, he doesn't move. Instead, he stays rooted in place, watching me go with Viktor.

The drive home is quiet. We don't even put the radio on. Viktor keeps glancing over at me. I'm sure trying to gauge my level of anxiety.

We finally pull up at home. The adrenaline's worn off, and I'm exhausted.

"Do you want a snack?" Viktor asks when we get in the house.

"I don't think so." I yawn. "I'm so tired I think I'm just going to go to bed."

He looks a little disappointed. Our regular after-show routine is to come home and have a snack. Sometimes we watch a movie or go for a walk on the beach, but tonight I'm spent.

"No problem. Sleep well."

I walk down the hallway to my bedroom and change into a nightshirt. I don't think my head hits the pillow before I'm asleep.

Amelia

I'M STARTLED AWAKE BY THE SOUND OF SOMEONE yelling and banging on the front door. I grab my phone and see it's three a.m. I jump out of bed and throw open my door. Viktor's already in the hallway, gun in hand.

"What's going on?" I ask him frantically.

"I don't know. Get in my room and lock the door," he orders.

I'm frozen in place. The sound of yelling grows louder and more desperate."

"Amelia." Viktor shakes my shoulder, getting my attention. "Go. Now."

I run into his room and lock the door. Then, I tuck myself on the floor between his bed and the wall.

Viktor

THIS IS MY WORST NIGHTMARE COME TRUE. SOMEONE'S found us, and now Amelia's in danger. I wait until she's in my room, and I hear the click of the lock before I go to the door. With my gun in hand, I look through the peephole to see who's on the other side. My anxiety subsides when I see who it is, and I tuck the gun in my waistband before undoing the locks and opening the door.

"Mateo, what are you doing here?" I drag the obviously drunk kid into the house. "You're lucky the neighbors didn't call the cops."

"I came to see my girlfriend." He slurs his words. "Amelia," he calls.

"Shut the hell up." I take him by the arm and sit him down on the sofa. "Why do you want to see Amelia?"

"To tell her I'm in love with her."

"Mateo, you're drunk. You have no idea what you're saying."

"I might be drunk, but I still love her." He points a finger at my chest. "I know you do, too, but you can't have her."

What the hell is he talking about? Me? In love with Amelia?

"Mateo, you're drunk. You have no idea what you're saying."

"You can't have her because you're an old man." Mateo

laughs. "Where is she?" He tries to stand up, but I push him back down.

"Sit here and be quiet." I pull out my phone. "I'm going to get you a ride. You need to go home and sober up."

"I want to see Amelia."

"Not tonight. When you're sober, I'll consider it."

Thankfully, it's only a few minutes until a car appears outside. I walk Mateo out and give the driver his address. I wait until they pull away before going back into the house.

After I lock up, I go to my room to let Amelia know everything's okay.

"Amelia, it's me. Unlock the door." There's no response, so I try knocking. "Amelia, everything's okay. Come open the door."

I wait, and still nothing. When I listen closer, I hear her crying. Dammit. If she's not going to open the door, I'm left with no choice. I kick the door in. The sound of wood cracking is loud. Her scream is even louder.

I rush across the room and find her curled up on the floor next to my bed. "It's just me. Everything's okay," I say as I slide down and sit beside her. But it's like she isn't hearing me. She has her hands wrapped tightly around her legs. She's shaking and crying. "It's okay, Amelia. I'm right here." I use my finger to gently turn her head to look at me. "See, it's just me. You're safe. Breathe with me. Remember how we do that?"

She nods slightly and keeps her eyes locked on mine while we inhale slowly and exhale together. It takes several minutes before she starts to relax and her breathing regulates.

"Are you okay now?"

She turns to face me. I think she's going to say something, but instead, her lips meet mine, and we kiss. It takes a minute for my brain to catch up and fully comprehend what's going on. When I can think straight, I take her arms and push her away.

"What was that?"

"I kissed you," she says quietly.

"I got that much." I stand and start pacing.

Slowly, Amelia stands and watches me, but she says nothing.

"Sit down." I motion for her to sit on the edge of my bed.

"I know I don't have a lot of experience. Do I kiss that bad?"

"Amelia, it's not that." I sit next to her. "It's just— We can't do that. I'm too old for you, and most importantly, I work for your father. We can't have anything like that between us."

"Why not?" As soon as the words leave her mouth, darkness shadows her face. "It's because of what happened to me, isn't it?" She jumps up to get away from me. "You don't want me because Moreno took me, and his men raped me."

"No, Amelia. That has nothing to do with it."

"It does. I get it. I'm ruined, dirty." She wraps her arms around herself.

Shit. How the hell do I fix this? "None of that's true. I don't ever want to hear you talk about yourself like that." I get up and slowly walk toward her.

"Then, why don't you want me?" Tears stream down her face.

"I'm not a good man, Amelia. You deserve to find a good guy, someone closer to your age. Someone not like me."

"You're one of the best men I've ever met," she says quietly.

Her words go straight to my heart and leave an indelible mark. But no matter how much either of us might want this, it can't be. "I'm glad you think so, but you don't know me." I tuck a strand of hair behind her ear. "I'll always be here to protect you, but we can't—"

I don't get to finish my sentence before she turns and runs out of my room. I follow her into the hallway.

"Amelia, wait."

She doesn't listen. She goes into her room and slams the door behind her. I try to open it, but it's locked.

"Amelia, open up."

"Go away."

I stand there for several minutes, listening to her cries. I've just hurt her in the worst possible way. My heart's torn. I want to bust into her room, too. I want to wrap my arms around her and tell her I want her, too. Woah. Where did that come from?

This girl is so off-limits. I'm thirty-two, and she's my boss's eighteen-year-old daughter. She's innocent and sweet. I'm screwed up—damaged beyond repair. The last thing she needs is a guy like me. All I'd do is complicate her life and bring more danger into it. I can't fall for the woman I'm trying to protect again.

I know all that. So why am I sitting outside Amelia's door thinking about how good her lips felt pressed against mine? How right it felt knowing she was thinking about me—only me. And the only person I was thinking about was her. Then, the look of devastation on her face when I told her no.

I'm so screwed.

I stay outside her door until her crying stops. Then, I drag myself back to my room, where I lie awake in bed all night, picturing only one woman—Amelia.

Amelia

For the briefest of seconds, Viktor kissed me back. It was the most incredible feeling in the world. I'm sure he felt something too. But then he pushed me away—rejected me. Is what happened to me too much for him to look past? And how do I get him to see me as more than Maxim's daughter?

I grab my phone and call Natalie.

"How was your show last night?"

"It was amazing. There were so many people."

"I'm so happy for you." She pauses. "You know you'll have to tell your parents, right?"

"Yeah, I know. I'm working on that." It's going to have to happen soon. "I called because I need some more advice."

"About this mystery man?" She laughs.

"I kissed him last night."

"And?"

"It was perfect. Magical. Until he pushed me away."

"Why did he do that?"

I have to choose my words carefully. "He doesn't think the timing's right. We spend a lot of time together at school and band practice." That's all true. "I think he might be afraid people won't be happy if we're together."

"That makes sense. Your bandmates would probably be concerned that the band would suffer if you and he broke up."

"Mhm."

"But you really like him and want to be with him anyway?"

"Yeah." I blow out a frustrated breath. "What do I do?"

"Maybe try some group activities. Something light and fun. A game night or pizza and a movie with some other friends," she suggests.

"That sounds like a good plan."

"If things do get more serious, you may have to sit down with the other band members and have an open and honest discussion. Listen to their concerns and address them the best you can."

"Right." Time for a subject change. "How are you feeling?"

"I have a whole lot more morning sickness this time around."

"Pregnancy does not sound appealing to me."

"You'll change your mind one day."

Will I? Although the idea of little brown-haired, blue-eyed babies makes me smile, I'm not sure I want children.

"Thanks for the advice. I have to get going."

We hang up, and I shower quickly before going to the kitchen to face Viktor. I'm nervous, especially after last night. But, when I get out there, Viktor's sitting at the table nursing a cup of coffee.

"Hi." My voice is barely a whisper.

"Hi."

"About last night. I'm sorry. I don't know what I was—"

"It's okay. It was a stressful situation. We're good," he says, never looking up from his coffee.

"Mateo and I are meeting with some friends to grab a bite to eat and catch a movie later."

"Is he picking you up?"

"No. I told him I'd meet him there." I reach into the cupboard to grab a cup and make myself some coffee. "You never told me who was at the door last night." I take my mug and sit across from Viktor at the table.

He looks confused. "Mateo didn't tell you?"

"Tell me what?"

"It was him. He'd been drinking. He was really drunk." She looks concerned. "I got him a ride and sent him home."

I didn't know Mateo drank. He's not twenty-one yet, but I don't have to remind Viktor. He already knows.

"It must have slipped his mind." I shrug.

I can't believe it's November, and we can still wear shorts. Back home, it's already snowing. But here, the sun's shining bright, and there's not a cloud in the sky. Viktor and I spend most of the afternoon on the beach. I didn't want to come in, but we have to get ready for my fake group date tonight.

I'm walking a fine line by not telling him the truth, and I feel guilty for lying to him. The truth is on the tip of my tongue while we're driving. But I know after last night, he never would've agreed to it.

"What do you think about starting your driving lessons now that you've got your permit?" Viktor asks.

Because I'm not a United States citizen, getting approved for a learner's permit was quite a lengthy process, but it finally came in the mail this week.

"I'd love that."

"How's tomorrow after school? Or do you have band practice?"

"We're off this week."

"Perfect." He smiles.

I love his smile. He has a dimple on his left cheek. His eyes used to be sad all the time, but lately, they sparkle. He looks happy.

We pull up at the pizza restaurant and go inside.

"I don't see anyone yet," I say and look around. "Should we grab a booth?"

"Sure. I'll sit with you until they get here."

We order sodas while we wait. After a half hour, no one showed up. It's not a surprise to me because no one was invited.

Viktor checks his watch for the millionth time. "Weren't they supposed to be here a while ago?"

On the way here, Mateo texted me to ask if he could come over tonight. I use now as a good time to respond.

Me: Tonight's not a good night.

Mateo: We really need to talk.

Me: Now's not a good time. I'll talk to you tomorrow.

"They aren't coming."

"What?"

"Mateo fell asleep. His buddy texted him, but he didn't hear his phone, so they figured we weren't interested. They changed plans and went to the waterpark instead. Mateo isn't coming either."

"He's just going to stand you up?"

"He said he isn't feeling well."

"Maybe it's the amount of alcohol he ingested last night," Viktor says sarcastically.

"I'm sorry you had to wait here with me for nothing. I guess we should pay for the sodas and go home." I drop my shoulders.

"I don't think so."

"What do you mean?"

"We're already here. There's no reason not to order a pizza and watch the movie."

"Really?"

"Sure."

We finish eating and make it to the theater just in time. The previews are starting. Viktor walks me to our seats and then goes back out to get snacks and drinks. The last preview is just finishing up when he gets back. He passes me a soda and a bucket of popcorn while he unloads several bags of candy from his pockets.

"It looks like you bought one of everything," I whisper.

"I didn't know what you'd want, so I got a variety." He grins.

I grab the bag of chocolate peanut butter candies. "These are my favorite."

While we watch the movie, we share the bucket of popcorn, our hands occasionally brushing against each other. My stomach does flip-flops each time they make contact. I sneak glances at Viktor to see if he's as affected as me, but his expression gives no clue to his feelings—or if he even has any.

Although it's late when we get home, the sky is clear, and the moon shines bright.

"I think I'm going to take a walk on the beach. Want to come?" I slide my sandals off and set them on the steps to the house.

"Give me a minute to go put this in the house." He holds up the candy. "I'll be down in a few minutes."

"Okay." I start walking away.

"Don't go in the water alone," Viktor calls.

"Yes, boss."

Viktor

I needed a few minutes to clear my head. I knew from the start there were no plans with Mateo. He'd already texted me to apologize for last night and to let me know he was waiting to hear from Amelia about whether he could come over.

I was going to say something but decided not to. Why? Because I enjoy being out with her. I didn't want to share her with Mateo and his friends. But that's wrong. I shouldn't enjoy it. I can't want her, and I can't let that happen again.

I toss the leftover candy onto the kitchen counter and then open the glass doors. Stepping onto the balcony, I lean on the rail and watch her. The moonlight shines on her like a spotlight. Amelia's standing at the water's edge, her hair blowing in the breeze.

She doesn't realize how beautiful she is. How perfect she is for me. She consumes my thoughts. In another life, another time, we might be able to make something between us work. But in this life, if Max ever found out I have feelings for his daughter, all bets would be off. He'd likely hand me over to the Albanians himself.

Somehow, she got past my walls. She owns a piece of my heart. I stand up and sigh. As much as it hurts, nothing can ever come of it. I promised her I'd be down, so I leave the safety of the balcony and meet her on the beach.

"It's a gorgeous night."

She jumps. "You scared me."

"I'm sorry." We both stare out over the water, the waves barely visible.

Amelia steps closer, letting the water wash over her feet. "I have a recital coming up at school."

"You do? When?"

"Next Monday, before Thanksgiving break."

"Did you tell your parents?"

"No. I don't want them to feel like they have to drop everything to fly in for it. It's not a big deal."

"I don't think they'd agree with that. It's your first performance. They'll want to be here. You should call them."

Amelia pulls her phone out of her pocket and hits Irina's contact. She puts it on speaker. It rings several times before she answers.

"Good morning, sweetheart," Irina says. "It's been too long since you last called."

"Sorry, mom. I've been really busy with school."

"You must be by the water. I hear the waves."

"Viktor and I came for a walk on the beach. It's always so peaceful down here."

"Don't go in the water at night. I don't want a shark to eat you."

"I won't." She giggles. "The chamber music ensemble at school is having a recital next week. I wasn't going to bother you with it, but Viktor said I should call and let you and Dad know about it."

"Why would it be a bother?"

"I don't know." She shrugs. "The recital is only about an hour. That seems like not much for a super long flight. And I know you and Dad are busy."

"Amelia," Irina's voice turns serious. "We're never too busy for you. I'll speak to your father, and we'll make arrangements to fly in."

"Thank you, mom."

When they hang up, Amelia lets out a big sigh.

"I told you they'd want to be here."

"You'll still come, too, right?"

"I wouldn't miss it."

Amelia

MATEO PICKED ME UP EARLY TONIGHT SO WE COULD GO for dinner before the show. He brought me to my favorite sushi place. I asked Viktor to join us, but he declined as usual.

"When do you think he'll let me take you out without him tagging along?" Mateo asks, motioning to Viktor, who's eating dinner alone.

I watch Viktor for a minute before answering, "Never."

"Seriously?" Mateo cocks his head to the side.

"Yep. Viktor follows orders from my dad. And Dad says I have to have a bodyguard with me at all times."

"I can talk to your dad about it? I'll convince him I'm capable of taking care of you."

"Nope. That's not going to happen." I can't take my eyes off Viktor.

His shoulders are slumped, and he's scrolling on his phone. We always eat together. But here, he's alone.

"What happens if I marry you? Would you still have to have a bodyguard?"

His question catches me off guard. "Did you say marry me?"

"Yeah. Well, not right now. But maybe someday."

Mateo and I aren't even dating, and he's talking about

marriage. I think he and I will have to have a serious discussion, but not here. "To answer your question, I'm not ready to talk about marriage, but yes, I'd still have to have a bodyguard."

"What exactly does your dad do?" he asks, setting down his chopsticks. In Russia, everyone knows who and what my dad is. I wasn't prepared for this. "He's involved in some cutting-edge clean energy things. I really don't understand most of it." I shrug.

"He must be really rich or something if you need all this."

"Something like that." I don't want to continue the line of questioning about Dad's job, so I change the subject. "Tell me more about what these A&R people do. How will we know who they are?"

"Are you ready for tonight's performance?" Mateo asks while we're sitting in the green room.

I've never been so nervous about a show before, but tonight's a big night for Death Rat. We're playing at the Viper Room. We also have confirmation there will be several A&Rs in the audience. If all goes well, tonight could be the big break we've been waiting for.

On top of that, Mateo and I are premiering the duet we've been secretly rehearsing in the soundproof studio at school. Our professor was nice and let us bring the other guys in to rehearse, too. But, outside of the four of us, no one has heard it yet.

"I'm terrified."

"Listen, Amelia. I'm sorry about last week. You know, coming to your house like that."

"It's no big deal."

"It is to me," he says.

"How did you get served anyway?"

"Getting alcohol is surprisingly easy when you're in the band.

They don't even ask." He shrugs. "I don't usually drink that much."

"Why did you then?"

"I was jealous."

"Jealous?"

"Yeah. I saw the way Viktor was looking at you. When you left with him, you were holding his hand."

I'm really not sure what to say. I'm not going to apologize for leaving somewhere when I was uncomfortable.

"Amelia, I'm falling in love with you," Mateo confesses.

My heart stops. I had no idea he felt this way.

"Wow. Um," I stumble over my words.

"You guys ready?" Tristan asks as he walks by. "It's showtime."

I turn to follow Tristan onto the stage.

"Amelia, wait." Mateo grabs my arm and pulls me into him. "Please tell me you feel the same." He leans in to kiss me, but I pull away.

"Can we talk about this after the show?" My thoughts are spinning out of control.

"Of course."

I push my conversation with Matteo out of my mind and get situated behind the keyboard. It's surreal knowing we're about to play in a club that's nothing short of a legend, and it's packed. I scan the audience, and like every show, Viktor is seated right in front. We exchange glances just as the concert starts.

We play our full set to an enthusiastic audience. While the piano is rolled out for our last song, Mateo steps up to the mic and addresses the crowd. He talks about how he's fallen in love and makes no mistake about looking at me when he says it.

Mateo grabs his acoustic guitar and perches on the stool next to the piano. With a nod, I begin playing Pink's "Just Give Me a Reason." The first verse is my solo. I glance up and see Mateo watching me sing, but I avoid his gaze.

As we move into the chorus, my gaze goes to the audience. To a man with crystal blue eyes who's watching me intently as I sing about two people who bear the scars of their pasts but aren't broken. Two souls who've been drawn together to help one another learn how to love.

Our eyes remain locked on each other for the rest of the song. He has to know I'm singing about us. Tears drip down my cheeks and land on the piano's keys as I sing about the devastation in both of our pasts. About the parts deep inside that we thought were broken and the strength we share. The capacity we have to love again. It can't be denied. Viktor and I are one another's destiny.

We finish the song, and the room erupts in applause. We receive a standing ovation. Mateo approaches the piano and takes my hand, leading me to the center of the stage to take a bow. Then he wraps his arms around me, holding me tight against him. He's whispering something to me, but I don't hear what he says. All I see is the murderous look on Viktor's face and the clenched fists at his side. He makes an exit from the audience and heads for the stage door.

Backstage is pure chaos. Several of the A&R reps have made their way back. And there are women everywhere draping themselves over Tristan and Quincy. Thankfully, no one's interested in me.

I look for a quiet corner while I wait for Viktor. He knows I get overwhelmed by crowds, so he always hurries back. But it's taking him longer than usual because of how crowded it is back here. I make myself as small as possible while I wait. Then, finally, I see him heading in my direction.

"What did you think about the song?" Mateo appears from out of nowhere.

Viktor's eyes are locked on mine. "It was perfect. Amelia has a beautiful voice."

My heart's pounding. My body responds to Viktor's nearness.

Mateo steps in front of me. "I'd like to talk to you for a minute, Viktor."

"Go ahead."

Mateo glances at me and then back to Viktor. "It's private. Can we talk in the green room?"

"Are you doing okay?"

I nod.

"Wait right here. I'll only be a minute."

The two men enter the green room, closing the door behind them. I have no idea what's going on in there.

"Amelia, are you okay?" Quincy asks. "You're white as a ghost."

"There's a lot of people back here tonight."

"Where's your bodyguard?"

"He's in the greenroom with Mateo."

"That guy's got it bad for you." Quincy laughs.

"Viktor?"

"No, silly. Mateo."

"Oh yeah, Mateo." I manage a small smile.

"Want me to wait with you until Viktor comes back?"

"I'd really appreciate that."

Quincy and I exchange small talk while I wait for Viktor to come back.

Finally, the door opens, and they walk over to me. Mateo takes my hand in his.

"I got permission from your bodyguard to take you out tonight," he says.

"Only if that's okay with you," Viktor adds.

"I was looking forward to going home."

"The whole band was invited. I won't keep you out for long." Mateo rubs my hand with his thumb. "And you did promise we'd talk after the show."

We do need to have an important conversation. "As long as it's not for too long."

"Keep your phone on," Viktor instructs. "I won't be far away if you need me."

Amelia

"Where are we going?" I ask Mateo as we walk out to the parking lot.

"Tristan's having a party at his house. I can't wait to show you off to some of our other friends."

"How did you get Viktor to let me go with you?" I ask, looking over my shoulder at Viktor, who's walking a short distance behind us.

"I told him exactly how I feel about you." Mateo grabs my hand and threads his fingers with mine. It feels awkward—wrong." He said as long as he followed us and was inside the house for the party, we could go."

"Isn't that going to be weird? My bodyguard following us around?"

"Nah. It'll be fine."

Mateo opens the car door, and I slide in. I watch as he and Viktor talk for a minute, then Mateo gets in the driver's seat, and we're on our way.

"Can't we just go back to my house and watch a movie?"

"What do you mean?" Mateo glances in my direction.

"I'm not a fan of parties and crowds." We've talked about this. He puts his hand on my leg. "You'll be fine. I'm here."

"Mateo, I think we need to talk."

"I understand if you can't say the words back to me yet."

"Mateo, I—"

I stop talking when he pulls the car over in front of a house that's crawling with people and then shifts in his seat. "Don't say anything yet."

"I don't think—"

"Give me a chance to show you what we can be like. Let me make tonight special. We can talk about it later." His eyes plead with me to say yes to him.

I don't know what to do. I'm so confused. "Okay," I say quietly. I'm not comfortable ignoring this, but I also don't want to hurt him. He's a really nice guy. But he's not the one for me.

Amelia

TRISTAN'S HOUSE IS ENORMOUS, AND PEOPLE FILL
every nook and cranny. Mateo brings me from group to group
and introduces me to all his friends. Some I've met, but most I've
never seen before.

I smile and make polite conversation, but on the inside, I'm
freaking out. Somehow, I have to keep it together because I refuse
to have a panic attack in front of all these people. It takes all of my
willpower to keep myself grounded. What's making me more
nervous is that I don't see Viktor anywhere.

Mateo leads me to the kitchen, where pizza boxes are stacked
high, along with several different selections of alcohol.

"Want a drink?" Mateo offers me a can of beer.

"Umm, no. And you shouldn't be drinking, either."

"Loosen up a little." He pushes the can into my hand.

I take the can but don't intend to drink it. I'll ditch it somewhere before Viktor sees it. It won't end up good for anyone.
Mateo takes my free hand and leads me to a set of stairs.

"Where are we going?"

"Upstairs. It's a little quieter, and we can talk."

He knocks on a few doors until he finds a room that's not
occupied.

"After you." He motions for me to go into the bedroom first.

"I'd rather go somewhere else to talk."

"It's quieter here. You trust me, don't you?"

So far, he's not given me any reason to distrust him. Maybe he's right. I can't look at every guy as though they're out to hurt me. That was my past. This is my present. I decide to give him the benefit of the doubt and walk into the room. Mateo follows behind me, shutting and locking the door.

"Do you have to lock it? Can't we keep it open?"

"It's okay, Amelia. I'm not going to hurt you. I don't want anyone barging in on our conversation."

I'm uncomfortable with this, but I know Viktor can't be far away.

Mateo takes the beer from my hand and sets it on the dresser. "Come sit with me." My body's tense. Something doesn't feel right. "I know you've had bad relationships in the past, but that's over. You have me now." He tucks a stray curl behind my ear before leaning in to kiss me.

I let him. I try to make myself feel something other than friendship. But there's nothing. Then, he grabs the bottom of my shirt and tries to slide it up.

"No." I push away and jump up from the bed, putting distance between us.

"Don't you want me?"

I know he's had a rough life. He's alluded to things but hasn't told me his story. I haven't pushed because I know what it feels like to want to keep a part of your life secret. I have hidden scars I'm not ready to show the world as well.

"Mateo, you're a really nice guy, and I enjoy hanging out with you."

"Please don't do this, Amelia." Tears fill his grey eyes.

"You've helped make my transition to California so much easier than it would've been on my own. I treasure our friendship, but I'm not in love with you."

He stands up and walks over to me. "You may not love me

right now. Give me a chance. Let me show you how good I can make you feel. How good we'll be together." He grabs my hands and tries to lead me back to the bed. "Please say yes. I can't lose you."

Tears begin streaming down my face. "Mateo, I can't keep pretending. It's not fair to either of us. But you're not going to lose me. We'll always be friends."

"Friends." He wipes his face with the backs of his hands. "Is it because of Viktor?"

"No. Yes. I don't know." There are so many thoughts and feelings running through my head at warp speed that I can't manage to form a coherent thought. "I have feelings for him, yes. That's part of what I need to work through before I can move forward."

"He's a lucky man," Mateo says sadly. Then, he grabs his beer and walks out of the room, leaving me alone.

My whole body's shaking. I can't go back out there, so I sit on the bed. Every emotion I've experienced tonight rushes to the surface all at the same time. I don't hold back. I allow myself to feel and purge everything.

The door cracks open. I expect it to be Viktor, but instead, it's Sparrow.

"I thought I heard someone crying in here. Are you okay?" Sparrow asks as he walks over to me. "Never mind, that was a dumb question."

I manage a small smile.

"Wanna tell me what happened?"

"It's Mateo. He wanted to—" My voice catches on a sob. "He told me he loves me."

"Woah. I didn't realize you two were that serious about each other."

I'm glad Sparrow said that. It means I'm not the only one who missed it.

"I didn't either. I told him I didn't feel the same way." My tears start to fall again.

Sparrow grabs my shoulders. "Did he hurt you?"

I shake my head. "No, he just walked out. I don't think he's okay, but I can't go out there and look for him like this. I don't know where Viktor is. I want to go home."

"I haven't seen Viktor," he says. "But I can take you out the back way and bring you home if you'd like."

"Would you?"

"Sure. Come on."

Sparrow takes my hand and brings me down the hall to an elevator. "It's the staff entrance. No one will be back here."

He's right. The area's deserted.

"Are you okay with waiting here while I get my car?"

"Yeah. I'll be fine."

Within minutes, Sparrow's pulling up in a beat-up old Jeep. He gets out and walks around to open the door for me. "Sorry, it's not one of the fancy cars you're used to driving around in."

"I don't care about that." I smile.

Sparrow takes a narrow road that runs through the property until we reach the main road.

"Before we get too far, I need to text Viktor so he knows I'm leaving." I go to reach for my phone in my pocket. "My phone's gone."

"We can go back in and look for it."

I try to think back to when I last had it. "I put it in my bag that I left in Mateo's car."

"We can find him and get his keys."

"No. I don't think he wants to see me again tonight. I can get it another time."

Viktor

Mateo let me know he told Amelia he loved her before the show. He told me she was receptive to it, but that doesn't sit right with me. There was something else in her eyes when she sang that song. It was as if she reached inside me and pulled my darkest fears out, replacing them with her.

Could two people truly be destined for one another—even if everyone else will think it's wrong?

I agreed to let him take Amelia if she was okay with it. She was apprehensive, but she agreed.

I've been trying to keep my distance. I want Amelia to have the space to be an ordinary college girl. If something is up here, I'll know it. Kids have been coming in and out of the kitchen with pizza and drinks, so it didn't concern me when Mateo brought her in.

But that was over a half hour ago. There's no way they're still in there. So much for giving her space. I walk into the kitchen and look around. Empty pizza boxes are thrown everywhere. Beer cans and liquor bottles line the counter. But there's no sign of Amelia or Mateo. Where did they—

That's when I spot the back staircase. "If he touches her," I growl as I take the steps two at a time. The hallway's lined with doors. Much to the dismay of the inhabitants, I throw each door open in my search for Amelia, but she's not in any of them.

I pull out my cell to trace her phone. The location is just outside the house. Realizing I lost my shit for nothing, I take my time following the signal, which leads me right to Mateo's car. But there's no Mateo or Amelia. What the fuck? Her phone must be in her bag that's on the backseat. There's no way she'd leave here without telling me.

I search each floor of this oversized house but find no trace of Amelia. The last place I look is the backyard. There are kids everywhere. I check the pool area, but she's not there. My eyes scan the perimeter, and that's when I spot Mateo leaning against a tree.

I run over to him. "Where's Amelia?"

"I don't know," he slurs. "You're supposed to know that."

"Are you drunk again?"

He holds up a bottle of vodka. "I think so."

"What the hell are you doing getting drunk when you're supposed to be with Amelia?"

"Amelia's with Sparrow."

"Sparrow?"

"Yep." He nods dramatically. "She left with him." (he put her in his car and left out the back way)

I don't stand around to wait for any more info from Mateo. I break into a sprint. If anything happens to her, so help me.

Amelia

"Not at all."

"How long have you known Mateo?"

"Since kindergarten." Sparrow chuckles.

"So, you know his story?"

"I do."

"I met his family at his sister's wedding. But that doesn't make sense because a few weeks after that, Mateo told me his dad died when he was little. That he and his mom aren't close. I know there's more that he's not telling me, but when I tried to bring it up, he pretended he didn't know what I was talking about."

"I'm surprised he said anything at all."

There's a long pause. Do I ask? Would Sparrow even tell me?

"I can see the look. You want me to tell you Mateo's story."

"I do." I need to hear it so I can understand the pain I see in his eyes.

"Mateo's old man, or at least the guy his mom said she thought was his father, overdosed when he was about four. His mom was also passed out. Mateo called 911."

Sparrow goes on to tell me when the ambulance and police arrived, they found Mateo dirty, malnourished, and living in a complete dump. They tried to revive his father, but it was too late. He was already dead, but they were able to save his mother. Child Protective Services was called. They took Mateo away from his mom and put him in foster care.

"That's right about when we met. School was just starting, and he was in my class." Sparrow smiles. "He was smaller than everyone and didn't talk much, so some other kids liked to make fun of him. I don't know what it was. Something about the look in his eyes like he was lost made me want to stand up for him and protect him."

He was there for about two years while his mom got clean and eventually regained custody. After that, the boys lost touch for several years.

"Then, one day, we were in seventh grade, and he showed up again but was in rough shape. He refused to speak and flinched if anyone got too close. My need to protect him was even stronger."

It took some doing for Mateo to let Sparrow behind his protective shell. When he did, the things he described to Sparrow were nothing short of a living hell. His mom had only stayed clean for a few months—long enough for CPS to go away. That's when things went from bad to worse.

His mom prostituted herself out for drugs, and when that wasn't enough, she did the same with Mateo. She sat by while men raped him so she could get her next fix. What saved him was a broken collarbone.

"The last boyfriend was violent. His teacher saw him in pain and sent him to the nurse, who recognized he needed medical treatment. They couldn't get his mom, so they brought him to the hospital. CPS met them there, and he was put back into foster care. But this time, he wasn't going home. They found his mom dead."

"Oh my God," I say quietly. My heart splits in two listening to this story.

"The foster family he went to eventually adopted him."

"Mateo's adopted?"

"Mr. and Mrs. Hart adore him, even with his issues. Unfortunately, over the past few years, Mateo's been spiraling out of control. He's been drinking and doing drugs. I'm pretty sure he's high tonight."

That explains the change in his behavior tonight. Mateo was never that forward with me. He always respects the boundaries I put up. But tonight, it was like he wasn't listening to me—wasn't hearing me.

"Do his parents know?"

"I'm sure they do, but he's an adult. If he doesn't want help, their hands are tied."

Sparrow pulls up in front of my house. "Thank you for trusting me enough to tell me all that. I know I hurt him tonight. Can you go back and make sure he's okay?"

"I'll always look out for him. I—" Sparrow stops abruptly.

I can see in his eyes what he was about to say. "It's okay. Your secret is safe with me."

Sparrow looks at me. I know the look. It's the same one I have when I'm weighing someone's honesty. "Amelia, I'm gay. I'm in love with Mateo. I have been for years."

"Thank you for trusting me with that." I touch his arm.

"No one knows I'm gay. I don't know what my parents would do if they found out."

"Your secret's safe with me." I give him what I hope is a reassuring smile.

"It's nothing I can ever act on. Mateo's not into guys. He'll never return my love."

"I know a thing or two about loving someone who doesn't love you back," I say.

"Your bodyguard?"

"Is it that obvious?"

"To someone who's watching." I place my hand on his arm. "Your secret is safe with me."

Sparrow walks me to the door and sees me safely inside.

I reach out and hug him. "Thank you for the ride home. I'm only a phone call away if you need to talk."

"I'll keep that in mind."

I watch as he walks away and then closes the door. I make it to the couch, where I sit, stunned by everything I just heard. My heart aches for the little boy who was hurt by the adults he should've been able to trust. But I know from my trauma that he won't be able to have a healthy relationship until he's dealt with it.

I'm also sad for Sparrow. Being in love with someone who doesn't return your love is a difficult place to be.

I'm startled when the front door swings open. An imposing and angry Viktor steps in, slamming the door shut behind him.

"Why did you leave the party without telling me? You left your phone in Mateo's car and let some guy drive you alone. I had no idea where you were. And then I get here, and you don't even have the door locked."

I can't do this right now. Without a word, I stand and hurry to my room, slamming the door behind me. Then, I lay on my bed and cry.

Cry for Mateo.

Cry for Sparrow.

Cry for me.

Viktor

I DIDN'T MEAN TO LET MY DAMN TEMPER GET OUT OF control, but she had me scared to death. If anything happened to her, I'd never forgive myself.

Slumping onto the couch, I take a few deep breaths. Amelia's here, and she's safe. That's most important. As soon as I get my emotions under control, I'll apologize. And then we're going to have to have a talk about Mateo.

Heading down the hall, I stop at her room. I knock, but she doesn't answer. I knock again. "Amelia, I'm coming in." I'm prepared for the door to be locked, but it isn't.

Amelia's lying on the bed. Tears drench her face. I sit next to her.

"What happened? Did he hurt you?"

She shakes her head.

"I'm sorry for yelling at you, but scared the shit out of me."

"I'm sorry," she says and tries to catch her breath.

"Are you ready to tell me what happened?"

"Right before the concert, he told me he loved me," she begins. "At the party, he brought me upstairs. He said he wanted to talk."

The same feelings I had when he showed up here drunk to

proclaim his love for her make their way back to the surface. Jealousy. Jealous that another man has feelings for Amelia.

"He started kissing me, and I let him. I thought I owed it to him to try," she says. "But then, he wanted more. He tried to take my shirt off."

"I'm going to kill him."

She reaches out and grabs my arm. "Please don't. He stopped as soon as I said no."

That sentence is the only thing saving that boy's life tonight.

"I told him we were just friends. That we'd only ever be friends."

"Why?"

"Because he's not the man I'm in love with. He's not you."

Her words hang in the air between us, and although I know I shouldn't, I lean in and kiss her. She opens her lips, allowing my tongue access. My hands tangle in her long hair. She lays back, and I place her arms above her head. Her chest rises and falls with her rapid breaths.

Our eyes remained fixed on each other as I remove her shirt, exposing her black lace bra. My hands explore her body and breasts before I lean over her and begin kissing her again. Her tiny hands take the hem of my shirt, sliding it up my chest. I sit up and pull it over my head, tossing it to the side. I need to feel her skin against mine.

She mewls in pleasure beneath me as our kiss turns more passionate. Her hands go for the button on my jeans, and that's when what we're about to do hits me. I jump back.

"We can't do this." I rub my hand over my head.

"Why not?" she asks breathlessly.

"This isn't right. I'm too old—"

"We're both adults, and we both want this," she says and sits up.

She reaches out for me, but I capture her hands. "Amelia, we have to stop. I'm sorry. I shouldn't have let it get this far."

I turn and head for the door.

"Please don't go," she cries.

I want so badly to turn around. To finish what we've started, but I can't. Without looking back, I walk out and go straight to my room, where I lock the door.

I sit on my bed and lean forward, my head in my hands. What the hell was I thinking? Why do I feel so drawn to her? She's eighteen years old. More importantly, she's my boss's daughter. Maxim would literally skin me alive if he knew I touched her.

I'm the last thing she needs. My past is dark.

I'm broken.

Everyone I love leaves.

Love.

I'm in love with Amelia Solonik.

Amelia

Viktor left so fast he didn't take his shirt. I pick it up and bring it to my face. It smells like him. My hands tremble as I pull it over my head. Why did he stop? I know he felt the same things I was feeling. I could feel how hard he was. He wanted me as much as I wanted him. And then he was gone.

I cry myself to sleep.

I was hoping I'd feel better after a good night's sleep. Maybe understand what happened last night, but I don't. This isn't going to be an easy phone call, but I have to talk to someone.

"Hi, sweetheart," Natalie answers the phone. "How was your show last night?"

With everything that happened last night, I practically forgot about the show.

"It went really well. The A&Rs were impressed." And hope I didn't screw up the whole band. "I need to talk to you about something."

"Anything. What's up?"

"It's about the guy I've been telling you about." I pause. "Last night, things started to get physical."

"Was it consensual?"

"It was perfect until he stopped. He told me he didn't think he was the right man for me."

"I'm sorry, honey. That must've been really hard."

"It hurt. Especially because I know he's the right man for me, and he knows it, too. He's just scared of our age difference and what Dad will say. But I don't care. I love him."

"I'm a little confused. I thought we were talking about the band guy. I didn't know he was so much older than you."

"It's not the band guy. It never was. Please don't freak out," I pause and take a deep breath. "I'm in

love with Viktor."

Viktor

I COULDN'T SLEEP LAST NIGHT. INSTEAD, I SPENT THE last few hours of darkness pacing. My brain and heart are at war with each other. One part, the sane part, knew to stay locked in my room. Far away from Amelia. The other part wanted nothing more than to go back to her room, tell her I'm in love with her, and finish what we started.

Hoping to clear my head, I took an early morning for a run on the beach. I've just returned, but my thoughts aren't any better than when I left. My feelings aren't any different.

I'm in love with a sweet, spunky, beautiful red-haired woman —the one woman I'm forbidden to have.

"I'm so screwed."

I need to talk to someone rational who'll tell me this is crazy and that I need to stay away from her.

Pulling my phone out, I dial the one person I can trust with this. It rings a few times before he answers.

"Hello?"

"Hey. It's me."

"Yes, it is." Alex chuckles. "What's up?"

"I need your help. Your advice about a woman."

"You met someone?"

"Yeah."

"You've been holding out on me. When did this happen?"

"I guess a few months ago."

"That's great."

"I'm not the right man for her. Nothing good will come of this."

"Viktor, you have to stop thinking you aren't good enough—"

"Alex, I'm in love with Amelia Solonik."

He came home believing there was nothing left inside him worth saving.

Then she walked into his life.

And suddenly, the most dangerous thing in the world wasn't losing everything.

It was wanting someone enough to risk it again.

Continue the Fire & Ice series in *Her Nightingale*.

Find Tara's Books Here

About Tara

Bestselling author Tara Conrad writes where passion meets peril, crafting dark, spellbinding romances that blur the line between devotion and destruction.

Inspired by the haunting brilliance of Edgar Allan Poe, her stories reimagine Gothic tales with modern sensuality and power.

Within her pages, heroines rise unbroken, villains fall beautifully, and the darkness always tells the truth.

When she isn't writing, Tara travels with her husband, meeting readers who have found pieces of themselves in her worlds.

She believes love isn't always light. Sometimes, it's found in the dark. 🖤

Acknowledgments

This section can be a book in itself. There are so many people to thank. **First, thank you to YOU—the readers.** I appreciate your willingness to support a new author and her stories. I hope you continue to enjoy my books—there's a lot more to come!

To all the Instagrammers and Booktokers who are always willing to share whatever promos and links I pass your way. You've all played a major part in getting my books in front of new readers. I hope to meet you all one day to give you a big hug and say thank you in person.

To my author friends. I don't have room to name you all. I am very thankful for each one of you who has mentored me, supported me, and become my friend. I don't have the words to fully express how very thankful I am for each and every one of you.

George- my Dominant, husband, lover, best friend—my everything. None of this would be possible without your unwavering support and encouragement. I am so glad we're able to be partners on this journey. Thank you for putting those twists and turns into my plots. Thank you for listening to endless rereads. Thank you for my amazing book covers. Thank you for my beautiful formatting. The list goes on and on. i love You forever and a day!

To My Kids: To all six of you (this includes both Jonathan and Jacob M.) I treasure you all. Your excitement for my career is so important to me. The fact that you always try to drop everything you're doing to be at my signings means the world to me.

Your love is the most important. Know that you are all very special to me, and I love you each dearly.

National Human Trafficking Resource Center 1-888-373-7888
TTY 711
Text HELP to 233733

ONLINE RESOURCES

www.dhs.gov/bluecampaign

polarisproject.org

humantraffickinghotline.org

www.ingramcontent.com/pod-product-compliance
Lightning Source LLC
Chambersburg PA
CBHW030924210726
48290CB00007B/2060